THE TRUTH ABOUT ALICE

ALTA HENSLEY

Thank you to Jay Aheer for the amazing cover! Also a big thanks to Maggie Ryan for editing and helping my book turn to magic! I also can't forget my amazing betas! You all know who you are, and I love you. And of course all the readers that have supported me along the way. I have the best team in the world.

DEDICATION

To Mr. Hensley.

ame time, algae meant death. Especially came to the Penna and the Cyans.

Penna, deadly activists of a frozen planet—oup of brutal warriors and not much more. ulture was one built and framed by science man evolution. The birth of the Penna may een based on intelligence and advancement, arly had ended with hate and destruction. es to some, and devils to others. From what d see, they didn't have a need for all life, n they argued the opposite. They only took, nd abused. There was no sense in preserving hey did not need, or land that did not provide veted blue-green algae. The Penna had one se, and that was to grow, harvest, and nate the production of the algae. It was the evolution and survival.

was rather simple science, actually. Algae red carbon dioxide. The more blue-green the Penna created, the more carbon dioxide hed from Wonderland's atmosphere. CO2 Wonderland warm… until all the algae sucked warmth away. So why did we need all the e? Humans had discovered the cure to insons, Multiple Sclerosis, Muscular trophy, Alzheimer's, and many other diseases. most revolutionary discovery, however, was blue-green algae held the answer to the cure

1

The crackle of smoldering flesh overspread the sky with a ghostly-colored haze—a reminder of those who had died and surely would forever haunt the land. We had won this battle, but I felt nothing but an almost suffocating defeat.

Taking a deep breath and staring at all the carnage around me, I finally got the courage to verbalize what I had wanted to say for months. "I'm leaving," I announced to another soldier, who was assigned with me to guard the remnants of the convoy until the cleanup crew came to collect materials and any parts they found useful. I couldn't really remember the soldier's name, not that it was that important. We were groomed from childhood not to get attached to anyone, and he was nothing more than another faceless soldier.

"We've been ordered to stay here until the scavengers come," he said in a squeaky voice.

He annoyed me.

"I don't care. I'm leaving."

"Leaving?"

I pointed at a dead body lying face down in the snow. "I killed that man."

"So?" The soldier shrugged and pointed at another bloody body staring up at us with lifeless eyes. "I killed that man. What's your point?"

"They didn't do anything to deserve this." I bent down and reached for my bow and arrows resting on the icy tundra. "I'm leaving."

The soldier tried to stop me from leaving my post by placing his hand on my chest. "You're going to desert? They execute deserters."

I shrugged. "They would have to find me first." I brushed his hand away and walked out toward the barren terrain of nothing but swirling snow, icy land, and freezing temperatures.

I walked a solitary passage from my deserted post—no longer willing to be a mercenary of the Penna. My wrecked body swayed slightly, dried blood of others crusted on my uniform and exposed skin. I had fought beside my fellow team of killers as a whole Cyan convoy was slaughtered by our merciless hands. They had only been trying

to deliver nutrient-rich alg
food.

For food.

How could we kill with
murder?

Enough!

The memory of the gore
in my soul, only to add to
many other battles I had fou
As a Penna, and a woman, I h
—to be a breeder, or to be a
or to destroy it.

I had chosen poorly.

Continuing my stride with
rippling in the air all around r
screams and the moans of t
echoing inside my destroy
Enough. I had had enough.

Marching forward, with th
thoughts pounding against my
down and saw a broken glass via
frozen algae clinging to the s
whatever glass wasn't already
bottom of my boot in resentmen
grind against the icy ground. Alga
the war. Algae—the cause of dest
the cause of the apocalypse. Algae

for every form of cancer. A defense against oxidation damage to red blood cells and plasma was where it all began.

Science had finally won. Or had it?

The demand for blue-green algae grew far beyond what the planet could yield. The only way the mass amount required could be produced was via algal blooms—a rapid increase in density of algae in the aquatic system. The water of Wonderland was by far more priceless than gems themselves had ever been.

Hence the Battle of the Waterbodies. Decades of war. Decades of death. Humans destroying each other as science destroyed Wonderland.

Two factions were eventually formed. The Penna and the Cyans. The Penna fought for science, and the Cyans fought against it. The Cyans harvested the algae for a completely different purpose. For food. Blue-green algae was the most nutrient dense food on the planet, and with Wonderland's climate changing at a rapid speed, the Cyans wanted all the algae to go toward the basic needs of sustenance.

So, as the Battle of the Waterbodies raged on, the planet launched its own war and the waves of annihilation began.

First wave: huge storms, heavy rainfall and flooding.

Second wave: snow and blizzards as the solar radiation vanished.

Third wave: permafrosted tundra plains, barren land, large moving glaciers relentlessly crushing any civilization in their path.

Fourth wave: Wonderland's thermostat all but frozen. The beginning of an interglacial period. An icy apocalypse, not quite merciful enough to take all human life, but rather keeping us all alive to be forced to live on this ruthless landscape.

Even through all this, the Penna spread throughout the icy tundra of a planet forever cast in a dark and deadly ice age, seeking only power and control of a commodity rarely found now that Wonderland had become a frozen ball of ice.

I was one of the Penna... until today. I had finally had enough. I could not condone this any longer. I believed in the Cyan way far more than I did the Penna. Science had destroyed Wonderland, and I was helping them in this quest. Or at least I *had been*. I would rather starve to death than watch another Cyan die before me.

A clash of swords reverberated in my mind and echoed in my heart. Guns and other forms of advanced weaponry had eventually been swallowed up by the ice age the same way Wonderland had, leaving us all in a medieval darkness of primal living. In the eyes of my fellow warriors, Penna—the most intelligent of humanity—were the only ones worthy enough to possess the algae and had been overcome by greed, power, and a fatal arrogance. That had to be the only excuse for their behavior. It was the only explanation for the death and brutal carnage caused by the mercenaries. For the Penna, the sort of bloodletting the Cyans suffered meant something more. The rapid coldness of each kill sent a message that the Cyans deserved no mercy for being the leeches of Wonderland. They were not worthy, and therefore should not exist on what was left of Wonderland.

I was a headstrong and righteous woman to any who knew me, with an unwavering spirit and an unwillingness to back down, no matter the odds I was facing. I was truly a threat. An archer by choice, I was rarely found without my bow at my side and a large supply of arrows at the ready. But I could no longer fight for a side I did not believe in. So I left. I simply walked away from the camp and into the snow that swirled all around me.

The withered remnants of a long ago battle surrounded where I trekked. The icy landscape was now riddled with what was left of death from so many wars—human bones picked clean by wild animals. A fire of pain swept throughout my sturdy legs, and yet I had no choice but to continue on.

There was no turning back. I inhaled a breath of blustery air as it gathered speed against my back. I held my hand over my watering eyes, desperate to shield them from the punishing sun and freezing air. After walking so long in the cold, I almost felt as though I'd been caught in a waking dream. The weight of my weapons hanging from my back filled me with an obscene sense of comfort so they would remain where they were, even though without them, the walk would have been much easier.

Avoiding the sting of the biting wind by squinting my eyes as much as I could, I spotted something dark teetering far away in the distance. I hunched down, moving my hands slowly over my shoulder to my back. There was nothing but broken pieces of frozen wood scattered about. Nothing of significance to hide behind. If it was the Penna thundering through the icy dunes, they would find me, ravage my flesh, and set what was left aflame—all in the name of Science... their science. I was now a deserter, a traitor, and their enemy. And if it was a Cyan, my fate would very likely be the same. Either way, I was alone without a side to call my own. But I would not die without a fight—that much was for sure. I would hold my head high, shoulders back, and I would maintain my pride as the metal of the sword pierced my flesh. My hope was that it was merely a scout whom I could kill before he would run and inform the others of my whereabouts.

Pulling a wooden arrow from my quiver, I nocked it, curling my fingers around the heron feathers, but seeing nothing but the steep tip on the other end. Now or nothing. I raised and drew in one fluid movement, teeth bared as a cold snake of fear coiled around my stomach. The arrow flew free from my steady hand, striking my target in the distance. Strangely, I didn't hear a yelp or a high-pitched scream. I ran forward, leaving footprints after each step. My knees sank into the snow at the side of my kill. Silent and reeking, the creature must have already been dead for some time.

A snow fox, a shrewd ice age creature, lay with half of its body exposed above the snow. I looked in all directions, laid my hand on its black shiny nose and stabbed it in the gut. All I felt I had time to do was fill my flask with its blood, and my starvation would hopefully be held at bay until I could find another source of food and sustenance. I closed my eyes and took a deep soothing sip, ignoring the bitter, metallic taste. Brushing the snow off my knees, I yanked my arrow from the thick shag of its hide and buried it in the quiver against my back.

When I turned to walk away, I stumbled as the carcass flopped down a man-made hole—a hole created to trap game. The fox had been set there by a crafty huntsman to lure animals to their demise. The stony snow rattled underneath my feet. I charged forward at lightning speed, but everything else appeared to stop, as if time had slowed down. Snow sank under my feet, and the earth crumbled beneath me. I fell into the trap, following the dead fox.

"No!" I screamed, as if anyone could hear my cries.

A shower of snow filled my mouth. My body lay completely still, but my thoughts scurried wildly in my head. A cool light covered my body as settling frozen particles cleared from the air. When the powder clouds evaporated, my mouth hung open in shock. A colossal sinkhole sent me down to my deadliest peril, but somehow I survived. My dark hair was tossed over my shoulders like matted rope, small scrapes, beginning signs of bruising, but there was nothing broken and I was still alive.

The only way out was up. "Fuck," I wheezed before eyeing my environment with hopeless wonder. I cursed under my breath again.

I scanned the hunter's trap, seeking something ready for me to grasp. Tension pumped through my bloodstream. Frustrated and frightened, I craned my neck to see out further. I closed my eyes and tried to regain my composure. This trap would not be my demise.

I glanced at a rope hanging from the top of the hole—no doubt for the hunter to use to retrieve his prey. My arms were too sore with potent agony to climb. A sense of panic tingled in the pit of my gut. The growing nightmare had my blood running hot like a fever. Or maybe it was the actual feeling of starving to death setting in. Either way, the fear of dying alone in this hole almost paralyzed me on the spot. My fate was to die in battle… or so I once believed. I closed my eyes again. But once I opened them, I tuned out the thoughts of terror blaring in my head, and found my inner warrior.

Taking a deep breath for strength, I managed to find my second wind and rushed underneath the swinging rope. I jumped and grabbing hold, wrestled up, locking my legs by the ankles. By now, the sun had started to set, and dusk was not far off the horizon. The knowledge that I would die here if I did not keep my body moving powered me on. I could do this. I *would* do this.

Before long, I had writhed my way to the middle of the frayed rope. Looking at my hand, I could see my skin was rather pale and sallow. Fear of fainting worried me, but I'd be damned to give up and die in this trap. I had but two choices: get out, or get buried in my new icy grave.

Everything around me shook and tumbled. The walls of the hole seemed to be on the verge of caving in. With the fear of an avalanche looming, I glanced up and plunged ahead toward the opening, toward survival. Briefly, I turned back to see the place that could have been my grave and gave a large sigh of relief. I would live. I would make it. I didn't survive fifty-two battles to die in a hunter's trap like a wild boar.

My aching hand slapped the top of the glacial surface, and then I just as rapidly heaved myself from the snowy depths. Dark, violet moonlight bathed my body, and a toothy smile spread on my face. I stared up at the path before me and refused to lie down any longer. Many obstacles had crossed my path, and this was just another one I had conquered.

I labored through the sparse and quiet vastness of the arctic land. With each step more excruciating than the last, I focused my energies onto why I made the impossible trek in the first place. My chapped, sunburned, and frostbitten lips cracked in the corners. My thoughts made me smirk. What would the Penna think if they found me? The once powerful mercenary, now barely walking, merely holding on to the life I had left.

I peered down at the shining granular crystals gleaming by full moonlight under my feet. I blinked hard, and this time gazed more intently at the snow. I stopped abruptly, crouching to press my hand against its soft surface. The impression of trek marks from a snowmobile was obvious in the grit. Very likely someone was waiting out there in the night shadows, stalking their prey, waiting to make the kill. I reached behind my back, grabbing my bow in one hand and an arrow in the other.

"Go on, come and get me. I promise I will make your death so grueling you'll wish I knew mercy!" I screamed my threat with as much force as my wrecked body allowed.

"Who the hell are you?" I heard a deep man's voice from afar call out.

"A *former* Penna. I come in peace." I swallowed back my fear and waited for him to reply. If they were the Penna, I would soon be dead for using the word *former*. But if they were Cyan, I would be dead for *not* using it.

Instead, I heard the snap of fingers. As calmly as if it were absolutely normal, men drove out on snowmobiles, once hidden behind scattered snowdrifts and piles of ice. A tall man, with dark brown eyes and even darker hair, drove up next to me and glared at me—a runty, snow-covered woman in comparison to his muscled build. I kept my eyes squarely on his outerwear, much heavier than any Penna would wear. The bulky weight of material needed for warmth gave away that this man was definitely not a Penna. My heart nearly stopped in my chest when I recognized who he was—a general in the army of Cyan. I stood tall and proud, but hoped I didn't look ominous and ready for a fight. I knew it was a fine line between enemy and victim, and I didn't want to be considered either. He had a regal arch in his neck and sat upright with a brooding glare in his eyes, and I knew he was sizing me up and carefully considering his next move.

"I'm no longer a Penna, and I'm just trying to find my way to a village," I said, practically holding my breath as I spoke.

An eyebrow rose as he asked, "How are you no longer a Penna? You either are one or you aren't."

"I once was, but my situation has changed," I countered.

He glanced at my bow and arrows and asked, "An archer?"

I nodded, a part of me wishing I had ditched my weapons long ago. At least then I could claim to have been a breeder rather than a mercenary, but there was no use in lying now. "Yes, a mercenary... or... at least I once was. But if you will let me, I would rather leave and never look back."

One of his men drove up next to him and said, "Rabbit, a fresh storm is setting in. We need to head back to the encampment before we get caught in it. Unless she's hiding food under her clothes, she is of no use to us. Leave that Penna filth to her own demise." The man looked at me in disgust. "Better yet, kill her now and put her out of her misery."

I bit my tongue to help fight back the urge to tell the man to go fuck himself, and as much as I hated to admit it, the urge to kill all Cyan still sizzled within my bones. I still had my bow and arrows and the high-level skill to slaughter these men before they even saw it coming, but I was done with that life. I did not want to be a Penna any longer, and murdering these men—or at least trying to—was the act of a true Penna mercenary. Yet I would not allow them to kill me either, so if it came down to it, another battle it would be.

My turmoil of thoughts was interrupted by a wail of screams of combat exploding far off in the air. Rabbit's two men drew their swords, scanning the area for the enemy.

"The Penna aren't far, and she may have led them straight to us. Take her," Rabbit demanded as he held his sword of blood-stained steel before him, poised for attack.

"She's a God damn spy!" one of the soldiers called out.

"Kill and gut her so her fellow Penna see what

happens when they try to trick us by sending a so-called traitor female our way," another shouted.

"I'm not a spy. I'm simply trying to find my way to a village. I swear this isn't a trap!"

Rabbit turned and stared at me with fury in his eyes. Getting off his snowmobile, he took a few strides my way and towered over me. His eyes studied every inch of my body, practically burning a hole into my very presence, as if the man was deciding right then and there if he should slice the blade of his knife through the flesh of my neck.

"Tie her up, and take her with us," he ordered. "Let's move out!"

Two soldiers grabbed my wrists, clasping my arms in a thick rope knot. One of them removed my weapons from my back and patted me down, finding all my hidden knives. They then yanked the bonds forward, dragging me every step of the way.

2

A hearty burst of chuckles greeted me when I arrived at the Cyan army encampment. Campfire reflected in the eyes of my captors. Torches all around gave a hellish glow to each of them. The sudden thud of a man's boot smashed against my weary thighs. I nipped my tongue, collapsing on the arctic ground. A low-voiced man grabbed my cheeks, squishing them in the palms of his hands as he raised me to a standing position.

"Do not see the fact that we haven't killed you yet as an act of kindness, Penna dirt." His heavy-lidded eyes washed all over my body. "Let me reassure you, all you are is the sex between your filthy legs. Trust me, I will take it as I please, and I'm afraid I won't be polite about it. And then, when I'm done, each man here will get his turn."

His lips were chapped and the tip of his nose showed signs of once having had minor frostbite.

I squinted my eyes, reading the Cyan soldier's thoughts as I understood exactly what was on his mind. I stood straighter and shouted for all to hear, "Try it, and I will bite off your pathetic cock and spit it out before your boots." It was a warning he should take seriously as I meant every single word of it.

The brute's eyes widened. He raised the back of his hand to my cheek. "Why, I ought to slap your mouth, you bit—"

"Enough!" Rabbit's harsh command mastered the night sky from behind us.

Rabbit's man released my chin but he gave me a long and livid gaze.

"You are a long way from the closest Penna post. What brings you this far north?" Rabbit asked as he pulled up in front of us, dismounted from his snowmobile, and stood before me. His height dwarfed my smaller frame. He tilted my chin with his finger so I stared directly into his dark eyes. "You say you are a Penna? A female mercenary?"

I nodded slightly. "Yes," I answered, once again fighting the urge to reach out and grab him by the throat and strangle him with my constrained bare hands. How many times did I have to answer the same damn question?

Another soldier kicked snow at me, spattering small ice crystals on my face. "She is not even worth a fuck. Penna are mutated freaks. You lie with one and you risk polluting your bloodline. She's just a shitty mutant."

I spun on my heels and kicked him in the shin with as much force as I could muster, and he just grinned as he shook the pain out from his leg. "Don't ever call me a mutant again." Even though he spoke the truth, I didn't like hearing the words leave his vile mouth. "I dare you to try to touch me." I held up my bound wrists for effect. "If I weren't tied, you would be dead right now."

Barks of laughter resounded. Rabbit waved his hand, silencing his men. He reached for my weapons on the back of his snowmobile and pulled an arrow from my dogskin quiver, strumming his index finger along the feathers.

"What is your name?"

"Alice."

He paused stroking the arrow to scan my body. He nodded. "And I am Rabbit White, commander of this army."

I nodded. Unsure if I should say anything else, I remained standing in place, in silence.

"And you actually know how to shoot one of these?"

I lifted my icy face upward. "I'm a better archer than any of your men."

Rabbit dropped his gaze, and we both made eye contact.

"Yes, well your arrows are so ancient and poorly kept, they stink like rotting wood. You are such a skilled warrior that you get caught marching through enemy territory. To be sure, does this sound like a warrior to you? It certainly does not sound like a Penna." He smirked and glanced at his men. "Rumor has it that the Penna are far more superior in intelligence than any other life in Wonderland." All of his men rolled their eyes, huffed or chuckled at the sarcasm that laced his words.

I didn't answer. Rabbit snapped my arrow in both of his two thick hands with no effort at all.

"You are just a little girl with too high a self-esteem." The men circling me snickered even more, enjoying the show.

Yes, I knew the role I was now in. The character I now played. I was his captive. His slave. I was at his mercy—if there was any mercy to give.

Rabbit stood before me with a mixture of annoyance and curiosity in his eyes. "It's time you tell me the truth. Why would you be wandering the tundra alone? Where are the rest of the Penna?"

"I told you. I left them."

"Explain to me what you mean by that."

I paused and studied the way his brow furrowed under his haphazard locks of hair. His authoritative posturing made it very clear he was not one to play around with. Manipulation, avoidance, or anything of that nature would not be a wise move on my end. I was powerless. My bow had been removed, and even the hidden knives I had tucked away in my boots were gone. I was certainly a scrapper, and could put forth a good effort in a fist-to-fist fight, but this man was double my size by a long shot. The solid wall of his muscular torso would likely break my hand if I even dared try to punch him. Rabbit wanted direct and clear answers, and he wanted them now.

"I don't want to be a Penna any longer," I said, wishing my words came out with more command than the pathetic squeak that oozed past my lips. Damn this man for scaring me.

He took two large steps forward, removing the distance between us. Pulling out a knife, he sliced the rope binding my hands, and firmly turned one wrist upward to view it better. "These feathers that mark your wrist clearly make you a Penna... and a mutant, as my man just said."

I glanced at my wrist and then looked back into his dark eyes as he studied the way the feathers blended with my skin. Never before had I been so ashamed of their presence. As a child, I was never given the choice if I wanted the multiple injections of cDermo-1. Every Penna began the process of mutation at the age of five. It was not a topic of discussion or a choice made—simply the Penna way.

Thanks to the Penna's ongoing science, they had discovered how to modulate the immune function in animals, and by combining the blue-green algae with cDermo-1, the Penna found the secret for warmth. Feathers.

Feathers could give humans what our own skin couldn't give us. Thermal insulation and waterproofing. The Penna discovered a way to inject cDermo-1 with blue-green algae into a human, resulting in a mutation. This mutation, or the materializing of human feathers, was the key to surviving the ice age. All the Penna had feathers along the surface of their skin. Not the entire surface, but in certain areas where warmth would leave the body, or areas to be used as a mark of status.

The Cyans disagreed again with this credence and act. They believed the algae should only be used as a superfood, and not used to mutate humans into what they considered a monster.

To the Penna, algae meant warmth. Warmth meant survival. To the Cyans, algae meant food.

Food meant survival. Both would do whatever it took to suck up all living matter that existed. To kill, to conquer, to win.

"I…" What could I say to his accusation that I was indeed a mutant? The Cyan people did not have feathers. They would never do such a thing to their bodies. Which, when you really thought about it, was a fair point—who would willingly mutate their bodies by injecting feather-creating toxins into the bloodstream? But to the Penna, it was once again the science. Mutation meant advancement. To them it wasn't about surviving the new landscape, but rather learning and finding a way to master it. Feathers were thermal insulation, and feathers were a natural way to water proof. Both were crucial to surviving the ice apocalypse. Once again, the divide between the Penna and the Cyans grew into an even wider abyss. Mutation versus natural.

"You are a Penna," Rabbit answered for me. "Plain and simple. So what are you doing here?"

"I left them. We had a battle, and I…" I paused while I tried to calm the quiver in my voice. "I decided today that I would no longer kill a Cyan again. I had had enough."

Rabbit's expression was impossible to read. His jaw tightened, his lips pursed. He didn't look angry, more pensive if anything. I was giving him things to think about. Would he kill me? Sacrifice me and make an example of what happens to a captured Penna? I thought his men certainly would like to see a spectacle be made. Would he send me back? Ransom me? Being returned to the Penna as a traitor would certainly be worse than death.

"What was your plan when you left the Penna?"

"Well," I licked my dry lips, "I planned on finding a neutral village and making a new home and identity."

He crossed his arms against his chest and huffed. "You thought it would be that simple? You would just walk into the subzero terrain in hopes of finding some village that you have no idea even exists? That was your plan?" One eyebrow rose and a small smirk broke the firm expression he hadn't eased up on until now. "You are a mercenary of the Penna, and you expect me to believe that you are foolish enough to just walk out into the middle of nowhere with no real plan?" He placed his hands on his hips and bent down enough that his face was in direct line with mine. "Who the fuck do you take me for?"

"She thinks you are a fucking fool," one of his men called out. He was the same man who had kicked me to the ground, and I made a mental note to kill him the first shot I got.

Rabbit looked over his shoulder at the man and

snapped, "Shut the hell up, Cheshire. I didn't ask for your God damn opinion."

Cheshire grumbled but didn't say anything further, but he did look toward the other men, who silently nodded their agreement. I really was screwed. The fact that the only man who was even showing the slightest bit of mercy happened to be the scariest one of the bunch, put me in the most precarious situation of my life. What would they do with me? Did he even believe my story?

"Where else do you have the feathers?" He wanted to know how much I had mutated, which made perfect sense. Feathers were a sign of class and power for the Penna. The more feathers you had, the higher up the ranks you were. Rabbit knew he could figure out how much of a Penna I truly was simply by the feathers on my body.

"My wrists, my ankles," I paused and swallowed hard, "the back of my neck, behind my ears—"

"Strip her," he commanded, growing irritated and impatient. I clearly wasn't answering as quickly as he wanted.

Cheshire grinned widely and didn't hesitate to move toward me. I took a step back and shouted, "Don't you dare touch me." If I had fangs, they would have definitely been bared for all to see. I was prepared for battle.

Cheshire paused just long enough to glance at Rabbit, who nodded his approval for him to continue.

Without another moment of hesitation, Cheshire charged forward and reached for the top of my arm. When I started to resist, two other men came in from behind me and held me still. With no use of my arms, I thrust my body back and kicked with all my might, making contact with my boot to Cheshire's chin. "I will fucking kill you!" I spat.

Cheshire touched his chin, took a moment to move it around to regain his composure, and yanked furiously at my clothes. In a flurry of me kicking, tugging, twisting, and resisting with every ounce of my strength, Cheshire and his men had me stripped completely bare, standing before Rabbit while he simply watched with zero emotion on his face.

The two men still held my arms and prevented me from doing anything but remaining in place before their leader with all of me to see.

Exposed.

Yes, he could see my feathers, but he could also see my breasts and the curls on my mound. He could see my nipples pebble as the cold air hardened them. The feathers would protect me from the harsh elements and freezing temperatures, keeping my inner core warm. I knew

I was in no danger of freezing, being naked, but that knowledge did not help my sense of rising panic in the slightest. Never had I stood nude before a man, and the wave of humiliation that washed over me almost took the breath right out of my body. His eyes felt as if they were setting me on fire. Very slowly, his gaze worked its way over every inch of my skin, and never once did the hard expression of Rabbit change. Nothing but solid stone as I wanted to melt in front of him.

"She has feathers on her lower back," Cheshire informed. It was his way of announcing that I indeed was a warrior. Only soldiers had the mark of the feather on the lower back.

"Turn her around," Rabbit ordered.

For a moment, I felt a sense of relief that he could no longer see my most intimate spots, and grateful he could only see the globes of my ass. That was until I heard him say the words that had me once again putting up my futile fight.

"Bend her over."

"Let me go!" I screamed breathlessly as I fought to no avail.

"Bend her over," he ordered again. The boom in his voice sent an involuntary shiver down my body.

The two men who held my arms and Cheshire worked together until I was bent over, staring at my toes. The frigid air made contact with the sensitive flesh between the flesh of my ass. I could feel the touch of icy air on my exposed pussy and my upturned butt, no matter how tightly I tried to clench my thighs together.

"Spread her legs," Rabbit ordered. I knew why he was issuing such a command. He wanted to know if I had feathers on my inner thighs, an indicator that I was at the very least a commander. I did not have feathers there, but knew he would not take my word for it without seeing it for himself.

Cheshire kicked my legs apart, and although I wanted to kill each one of them with the most torturous deaths I could think of, I didn't struggle any longer. I had lost this battle, and I needed to admit defeat... for now.

I could hear the heavy thud of Rabbit's boots as he walked up behind me. Seconds later, his fingertips ran along my inner thigh, feeling for any signs of feathers for himself.

"They aren't there," I said as I struggled to maintain my control. My body was betraying me, and the touch of his hand sent an electrical current of tantalizing pleasure straight to my core. Arousal blended with my humiliation, creating an erotic cocktail I wasn't sure I could resist imbibing. Such a simple touch, and yet such a powerful one.

Gentle yet firm, soft but hard, Rabbit caressed my flesh along every inch of my inner thigh. I couldn't hold back the gasp when, rather than lifting his hand and moving it over to the other thigh to check for signs of feathers there, he simply ran his fingers across my pussy in one slow, agonizing motion until he reached the other side.

"I told you that I don't have any feathers there," I said between gritted teeth. "I'm a mercenary. Or at least, I was one."

Rabbit continued to search my skin while his men held me in place. My back ached from being forcibly held in the position for so long, and my head felt light with the blood rushing to it and all the overwhelming sexual feelings coursing through me. The idea of Rabbit's touch made me sick, and yet my body disagreed.

"All right," he declared as he ran his final swipe across my pussy and then took a couple of steps back. "Chain her up until I decide what we are going to do with her."

"Damn you," I snapped. "I'm not a fucking slave to be chained."

Before I could continue with my verbal rampage, I was silenced by a painful slap to the ass. "Silence," Rabbit demanded as he spanked me again, and then again. "You will be whatever the fuck I decide you will be." He continued the onslaught of swats to my upturned bottom as he spoke, building in intensity with each one. The men continued to hold me in place while Rabbit punished me like a naughty child. "And you'd better learn that fast if you know what's good for you, Penna."

My head spun and my body ached, but it was nothing compared to the heat building within the depths of my core.

"I'll kill you," I yelled as he continued to spank my ass with even more force than before.

Rabbit laughed, followed by his men. "Oh I have no doubt you would try, my little Penna. But you will find that very hard to do as my chained pet."

He lowered his swats until he was spanking my upper thighs. It took all my will not to cry out in pain, but I would rather die than give him the satisfaction of knowing my bottom was on fire. Mortification raged inside of me as my flesh lit to an inferno of angry hornets. I almost moaned in absolute relief when he finally ended the punishing blows.

"Take her to the tent and chain her." He paused as the men allowed me to stand upright and turned me to face Rabbit, who had just treated me like an errant child. When my entire front was bared to him once again, he gave a wicked smile. "And keep her nude. After all, she is a Penna and has her feathers to keep her warm."

I tried to pull my arms free, but realized that resisting these men would get me nowhere, and I honestly didn't want to take the chance of a repeat session with Rabbit's hand. No, I would go with them. I would allow them to chain me. But I would plan. I would plot. And when the time was right—I would get my revenge and kill every last one of them.

3

I lay on the floor, chained by both ankles, falling in and out of sleep with the thunderous thoughts pounding in my head. My deepest fear had everything to do with being too meek, too gentle, and too weak. All my fears were clearly for nothing now since I was naught but a captive at Rabbit's mercy. Even if I wanted to fight, the metal securely holding my ankles prevented me from doing much of anything.

The darkest questions inundated my exhausted mind. What would Rabbit White do to me? Did he have a plan? Why hadn't he killed me? There must have been a reason for not doing what his men all wanted. All he had to do was slice my throat and move on, never giving me a second thought. Killing wasn't something he hadn't done before. You could not be a leader of the Cyan and not have killed. So why? Would he torture me for information that I may or may not have? I supposed I did have some information of value, although in all truth, I would offer that info to the Cyan with no need of torture. I would betray the Penna gladly.

I looked down at my wrist once held by Rabbit's powerful, large hand, and grimaced at the sight of my feathers. My fucking feathers. I hated them as much as the Cyans did. They marked me. Branded me. Forced me to be something—or someone—I wasn't. And now Rabbit and all his men had seen them. Exposing my feathers was far more embarrassing than exposing my flesh, though that had been mortifying in itself.

A breeze blew up the dark brown tendrils of my hair as someone rushed into my tent with a burning torch in his hand. "We've got early hours, Penna cunt." I backed away quickly and stared into Cheshire's darkened eyes. The heat of the torch flickered tiny embers onto my snowy floor.

"Where are my clothes?" I asked, my eyes stark and wide. "I need them to go outside." This fact wasn't the truth, since feathers were actually enough to weather the most brutal of storms, but I would insist on it anyway.

"Confiscated," Cheshire replied.

"You cannot just take what is mine!"

"It would seem we already did." Cheshire leaned in, lowering the torch too close to my face. "Rabbit chose to strip you bare and keep you that way, now didn't he?" He slid his thumb against my soft white throat. I didn't flinch or squirm. He then placed some clothing effects befitting a Cyan fighter into my lap.

"What are these?" I asked. "These are not my clothes."

"New orders from Rabbit. Put them on." He pulled out a key, knelt down, and unlocked the metal around my ankles, setting me free.

"Why? I'll look like a Cyan fighter."

"Maybe that is the point, Penna cunt. Maybe Rabbit wants to use and abuse you."

"He wants me to fight? Against my own people?"

Cheshire didn't answer but stood up and brushed the snow off his pants.

"What if I refuse?" I asked.

"Then you can stay here as a naked slave. The plan would still be to use and abuse you, but as a slave. It will just be using you in another way." He chuckled at his own sick statement. "The choice is yours. Be used as a fighter, or be used as a dirty sex slave. If you ask me, I would prefer you as a sex slave."

"You would," I mumbled, using the clothing to shield my nakedness from his eyes.

"Listen, Penna cunt—"

"Stop calling me that!" I spat.

The smile he gave me dripped evil. "Listen, *Alice*. I don't agree in the slightest with Rabbit's decision to see what you've got when it comes to fighting. But thanks to an ambush from some of you Penna fucks, we have lost a lot of good men. We need an archer, and I guess Rabbit thinks you can fill that spot."

"So he wants me to join you as an archer? To be part of your team?" I could barely comprehend the absurdity of what he was saying.

"Stop asking so many fucking questions and get dressed, or I swear to God I will chain you back up and fuck your tight little Penna cunt and make you a breeder whether you like it or not."

As Cheshire backed out of the door, I was seized by a sense of urgency. I could run. I could use this opportunity of freedom, escape into the storm, and hope they wouldn't chase after me. Not having the courage to do so, I jammed my feet into the heavy leather shoes and slunk into a too-large tunic. The fabric was heavier than any material I was used to, but it definitely hid any sign of me being a Penna. You would have to look really close to see any feathers, and with the wraparound for my neck, and the snow cap, no one would know otherwise.

Did I want this? Did I want to join the Cyan? Maybe so. Maybe I was meant to be a killer until the day I was killed myself.

Another loud noise drummed outside my tent. I approached the flaps, slowly folded them apart, and saw a circle of snowmobiles parading outside my door. Rabbit revved his snowmobile, further breaking the silence of the early dawn darkness with the growl of his engine.

"Time to battle," Rabbit said. "Your snowmobile is waiting."

Rabbit took off into the swirling flakes of snow, followed by the laughing rabble of his battle-weary soldiers. I moved to straddle what I supposed was to be my snowmobile, gripped the throttle hard, and drove close behind.

I knew I wanted to prove something to these men. My future depended on it. If I truly was going to go down this path and join them, I would have to prove my skill and earn their trust.

We all drove far from camp before stopping short at a jagged snowy cliff face. Cheshire dropped his burning torch in the snow, riding alongside Rabbit. The morning hours in the icy lands were so cold at times, it could easily kill the average person. But I was not average. No—my feathers and the cDermo-1 that flowed through my veins granted me the ability to not feel the cold.

"Where are we?" I asked.

Rabbit got off his snowmobile. "Time to show us you are ready to fight."

I couldn't help but gaze upon Rabbit and the way he gracefully dismounted the vehicle. In that small moment, it felt like I was seeing him for the first time.

"Who says I'm ready to fight? I told you, I walked away from all of that."

Rabbit crossed his arms and glared at me. "Cheshire?" he asked over his shoulder. "Did you tell our little Penna what her options were?"

"Yes, sir. I told her she could fight to her death or be fucked to her death," Cheshire answered.

Rabbit smirked and raised an eyebrow. "So since you are questioning fighting, I can assume you would rather choose the fucking option?"

"Of course not," I spat.

"Maybe she is a shitty fighter," a man called out from another snowmobile.

"Or a shitty fuck," Cheshire threw in.

Other men laughed and agreed.

"Fuck you all!" I screamed. "I could take each and every one of you if I chose to."

"So what do you choose?" Rabbit asked. "Fight or fuck?"

I swallowed back the rage inside and answered, "Fight. I'll fucking show you fools how it is done."

Rabbit nodded and raised his hand to silence all the laughs and taunts coming from his men. "Very well. As of this moment, I am your commander. Do you understand?"

I nodded.

"I expect to hear, 'Yes, sir' when I ask you a question."

"Yes, sir," I countered, feeling as if the words practically burned my tongue as I said them.

"If you want to survive a fight, you will have to master hand-to-hand combat."

I raised an eyebrow. "I'm an archer, I handle bows," I replied plainly. "Although I feel I have also mastered the sword."

As I dismounted, Rabbit waved to Cheshire to hand him my bow. Before he reached Rabbit's side, he elbowed me hard in the ribs. I stumbled off balance for a few steps. The other men stifled their laughter. When I lifted the bow out of Rabbit's hands and readied it, he pressed his chest against the raised arrow.

"All right then, try to kill me."

My first reaction was a breathy laugh in my throat. I then glanced in the eyes of the other men, looking for some sort of reassurance. It wasn't so much that I couldn't put Rabbit down in the blink of an eye. Instead, my biggest concern was how the other men would react to seeing his lifeless body fall over in the snow—red staining white. So be it —death to their foolish leader it would be.

I hesitated only a few seconds and then released my arrow. Rabbit threw himself back fast and the arrow sped out, piercing the dark. He grabbed the bow from my hands, spun around me, and slammed it hard against my buttocks. An electric sting of pain spread throughout my bottom. Again the bow hit me, this time against my upper thigh, causing me to lose my balance. I fell to my knees with my hand covering my stinging behind. Bruised pride hurt almost as bad as the quick punishment to my lower region.

Rabbit squatted next to my side, pushed me to where I was on all fours, and swatted my behind two more times. Fury mixed with humiliation nearly blinded me.

"Does this make my point clear?" he asked. "Just being an 'archer' is useless. A lesson for you. Fighting means learning how to brawl for your life. Especially when weapons are not an option."

Rabbit stood up and stretched out his hand to help me to my feet. Taking it, I pulled back a bit, forcing him to bend forward, and then punched him square on the jaw with all the force in my body. As he pulled back, I jumped up, slid to the side and thrust my foot out, kicking him in the backs of the knees, followed by a boot to the gut, leaving him to roll and fall near the edge of the cliff face.

The other men hurried from their snowmobiles and rushed to his aid. It all happened so quickly, they hardly saw the blow. Eventually, Rabbit came into his own again. He looked idly down into his hand, slowly wiped his bleeding lower lip, and smiled.

"You are much stronger than I thought."

"A lesson for you," I said. "Never trust nor show mercy to a Penna in battle." I winked, taunting him.

He stood up and brushed the snow off his clothes, shrugging off any assistance offered by his men. I stood ready for his retaliation and prepared for another round of battle. He took a long pause and scanned my body. "I have heard of a female Penna who can shoot a bow better than any man. So, if you want blood so bad you can taste it, I'll give you the chance to prove yourself. If for one moment I feel I cannot trust you, you will be killed without question. If you become nothing but a female burden in battle, I will let my men sort you out. Does that sound fair?" he finished.

I nodded.

"Have you already forgotten what I expect to hear when I ask you a question?"

"No, sir… I mean, yes, sir."

His lips quirked but he only shook his head. "I am not the commander you once took orders from. But my rules, my command, my authority, will be what you live by. If you falter, I will sort you out in my own way. Are we clear on the expectations of my army?"

I began to nod again but then quickly said, "Yes, sir."

I was surprised to see him smile and offer his hand for a friendly shake. "Welcome to the Cyans, Alice." He shook my hand and turned to the men. "She's one of us now. Treat her as such," he commanded. "Alice chose *fight*, so don't any of you dare choose the path of *fuck* for her."

4

The Cyan men had every reason to hate me. In their eyes, I was a woman and by nature, I was weak. The fact that I was a Penna made it even worse. If I wanted to join the Cyan ranks, and kill with the cunning power of the men, I would first need to fight like one. I had proven myself before, with the Penna, and I could do it again. These first initial battles would be my chance. I had left the Penna, but the warrior nature of my very being still burned bright. It was what I had been trained to do my entire life. Although I could walk away from the Penna, I could not walk away from my skill to fight. I knew I was meant to die on the battlefield rather than starving and barely surviving in some small village out on the tundra. Maybe this was my destiny all along—to join and fight with the Cyan.

I dropped to a crouch behind a mound of snow. Feeling tense with a sense of being watched, I scanned the surrounding land. Rabbit's army had left their outpost with two hundred men but now stood with fifty. The Penna had made fools of them. The men still thought it strange for a woman to fight among them, but Rabbit had made it clear that if they caused trouble with me, they were picking a fight with him.

Battle had proved my abilities. I stroked the bow I had mastered. It was heavier than some, but delivered the steadiness required for accuracy. I had taken it from the first man I killed in war. Two axes I had also claimed hung by my side. They were lethal for throwing, as one man who took me on had found. As I pulled out an axe, I stared at my reflection in the metal. My eye fell on the scar. Pale against the sun-kissed color of my skin, the scar stretched pink and red; a memorial of the last opponent I had fought. He had drawn a dagger and hurled it even as my arrow found his chest. If I had not seen it coming, it would have done worse than create a scar.

I crouched lower, movement catching my eye. I brushed my hair back. The dark strands always seeming to block my vision when clear sight was most needed. Three men on snowmobiles were riding just below the ridge, only the reflection of their helmets showing above the snow. I cursed, scrambling swiftly out of sight and sprinting back to the others.

"Enemies on the hills ahead!" I announced, sliding down the icy ridge to our evening encampment. Rabbit nodded, glancing over at the men. They were all tired. After three months of fighting, they had lost hope well before losing that final battle. With so few men, they could scarcely hope to avoid the enemy who would try to enslave or murder them. I knew the Penna well. The army of Cyan needed to regroup and make their way to safety, or die on the icy land.

"Alice, remain at my side. I value your aim. Men, get on your mobiles and prepare for battle. If those Penna try to take us, they will discover we won't be found sleeping."

Though exhausted, they had been trained to be instantly ready at the prospect of a fight, and the men scattered to their positions. I stood alongside Rabbit, my guardian and would-be protector since he had discovered that I indeed fought harder and better than any of his men. He acknowledged that I had mastered the art of the bow.

"Alice, get on your ride, and get ready to shoot."

I nodded, schooling my face to remain expressionless as a movement caught my eye. Four ice-covered hills away, a head poked above the snow then ducked down in a hurry.

"A scout," I said, keeping my voice down so only Rabbit could hear me.

He nodded before calling out, "They will be here soon. Be ready."

The men crouched down on their snowmobiles. They had already dug in for the night, so except for the narrow entrance, they were surrounded by a six-foot snow wall. The men also were in complete shelter as they prepared their bows or pulled out their daggers.

Reaching back, I grabbed my bow and strung it. The quiver was accessible, hanging just behind my right shoulder. Readying my aim, I waited for victory or death.

We did not have to wait long. Over the ice mounds and through the shifting snow charged a mixed body of men. Twelve had snowmobiles and the rest were on foot. I drew back my shaft, watching those on snowmobiles. As they drew near, the Penna raised a wavering cry and hurtled toward our defenses. One of the men came within range. I smiled as I released the shaft. The arrow sped true, piercing between the slit of the man's visor to send him crashing to the icy floor.

The other men reined back in shock. Few

fighters could fire a shaft as I could. The Penna had thought themselves safe. I smiled, loosing arrows at random among the advancing enemy, most of whom had left their faces completely unprotected.

I dodged an arrow and returned fire, taking out one of their archers. Their bows were often better than mine and the archers were out of normal range. They could not know that I wielded a stolen bow that was just as powerful.

I ducked below the snow wall to wait out a barrage of arrows. Grabbing two that struck near me, I popped up and fired the shafts simultaneously, and then ducked down without waiting to see if they struck. "They are close," I called to Rabbit.

He nodded. "Prepare for hand to hand!" he called, gripping the hilt of his sword. I made quick eye contact with him and nodded, drawing my sword and holding it easily in one hand.

I watched Rabbit, who had taken a quick look over the wall. He met my eyes, mouthing, "Three, two, one, now."

We both sprang up, followed by the rest of the men, whirling our weapons into the faces of our rivals. Shocked, the leading rank stumbled backward from their attack. Leaping the wall as the lust of battle filled me, I charged recklessly into the center of the fight. The axe clove torsos and dented helmets surrounding me. Dodging many of the blows aimed at me, I fought, releasing the rage and frustration of years locked under servitude to the Penna upon the unprepared enemy.

I faced off with one of the Penna men who had dismounted. As sword rang against sword, I realized I had fought my way through the enemy lines, and was now at the rear of the force. I was separated by the Penna from Rabbit and the Cyan soldiers, unable to aid or be aided.

I ducked a blow, leapt another, and spun into a whirlwind of blocks and parries. The man never let up, and I could not pause. A movement to the right caught my eye. Without pause, I switched to fighting one-handed with my sword and drew one of my smaller and lighter axes. Spinning rapidly, I blocked a sword coming from the side. Leaping back, I engaged two Penna. Now hard pressed, I permitted myself to be driven back. Keeping my eyes on the Penna, I observed a reflection in their helmets. Two snowmobiles stood behind me, by about ten yards I guessed, and just in front of them were the other two mounted men, prepared for kidnapping with a length of dark cloth.

As the man with thick feathers on his wrists thrust at me I dodged, letting the sword glance off my shoulder. Spinning sideways, I turned and ran for the two remaining mounted men. Quicker than thought, I hurled one of my axes at the man on the right while drawing my sword once again. The thrown axe flew true, striking the slits of the visor and hurling the dead man off his snowmobile. Planting one hand on the vehicle's windshield, I vaulted up. Drumming up the last of my energy, I kicked the other man in the chest. The force of my kick knocked him off the snowmobile as my sword found the center of his neck.

Twisting deftly, I landed on the recently vacated seat, and grabbed the dagger from his side pouch tied to the snowmobile. Spurring forward, I charged my earlier opponents, who were now nearly upon me. Dropping onto my back, I avoided a swiping blow meant to slice me in half. Twisting up, I hurled the dagger into the man's face. Turning the snowmobile, I charged at the remaining man who was trying to mount his comrade's machine.

Without waiting for me to reach him, he spun the snowmobile and dashed for the icy plain yelling, "Retreat, retreat!"

The sounds of battle suddenly ceased. Pivoting the snowmobile, I watched the men disengage from their defenses and run for the frozen abyss. As the last man disappeared out of sight, I swayed, suddenly light-headed.

Grasping the handlebars tightly, I leaned forward. My breath came ragged and fast. Glancing down, I realized I was wounded. Barely able to keep my balance, I slid off the snowmobile and leaned against its side.

Rabbit ran up, worry written on his face. I raised my hand, stopping his tirade before it could begin.

"I have a leg wound, and it feels like a few other scrapes and cuts. It doesn't seem that serious except for the blood loss and drop in adrenaline."

"Alice," he said, picking me up into his arms effortlessly. "You could have been killed! What were you thinking, charging off through the ranks like that?" He looked down and studied my bloody leg. "You're wounded, and you are a fool. If you weren't hurt, I would take a lash to your stupid backside and whip some sense into you."

"I fight. I may be a fool, but all fighters are," I retorted. His threat of a punishment sent a shiver through me as his arms tightened around my exhausted body.

Rabbit stopped walking and stared directly into my eyes, his breath warm against my face. An energy sizzled between us. I desperately wanted to look away, but refused to give him that power.

He shook his head and sighed, and continued walking toward his men with me held snugly up against his chest. "You are unlike any woman I have ever met; whose skin is as beaten as a man's and who bears the scars of combat. My men and I know your abilities and bravery, you proved that today, but you don't have to kill yourself just trying to prove to us that you are just as strong and skilled as a man. I know that. *We* know that."

"I don't know how to be any other way. I don't know how to be weak."

"I'm not asking you to be weak. But I am telling you that your need to prove your strength is going to get you killed."

"Then so be it," I mumbled as the throbbing of my wound beat at the same rhythm as my heart.

Rabbit's sigh was heavy as he carried me to an area where the wounded soldiers were gathered. "Someone clearly taught you the sword. Someone clearly taught you the bow. But someone clearly needs to teach you the art of submission."

"I submit to no one," I countered.

He paused and glared into my eyes. My heart beat so loud I was sure he could hear it. "And that attitude right there is going to get your throat slit. It's okay not to always have to try to be what you aren't. You aren't a man, Alice. You aren't a fool. You aren't weak. But when you try to be what you aren't —a man—you are a fool, and therefore, you are weak." His breath danced against my hair as he spoke. "It shows more strength to soften. To show that you don't always have that fake hard shell around you. I would have a hell of a lot more respect for you if you could soften and be true."

"I have no reason to submit, and I have no reason to soften. And frankly, I couldn't care less if I have your respect."

"You do want my respect." He smiled as if he was pleased he knew my deepest secret. "You have done nothing but try to show all of us that nothing can get to you. That you are indeed a warrior. I get that, Alice. I get that you are a damn good fighter. But I also see that your need to prove you are no different than any man is the chink in your armor. It makes you reckless and stupid."

"So by submitting and softening as you say, I would be a better fighter?" I huffed. "Do you tell all your men this?"

"No, I don't. But that's just it, Alice. They are men. You are a woman. Be proud that you are a woman. Don't try to hide that fact." He paused and looked at me, his features softening. "The fact that you are such a strong woman is very impressive. Just don't lose that part of you that makes you a woman. Don't try to be a man. You as a woman is far more powerful."

"You think I should be more womanly, is that it?"

Rabbit held my stare for a few more moments and tightened his grip around my tired frame. "Yes. You should." He continued walking without saying anything further.

I sighed, blinking against the dizziness that the blood loss caused. I took a deep breath to calm my nerves as he placed me on a blanket alongside the wounded men.

Five more men had fallen in the defense of our encampment, and another ten were seriously injured. From appearances, I was one of the less severely hurt, although the leg wound was rather deep.

Pulling up the edge of my pant leg, I let one of the soldiers clean and stitch the wound. I had another slight gash on my upper arm, and one across my face along the cheekbone. A few stitches and bandages later, I felt far better.

After everyone had been bandaged, I beckoned to Rabbit. "Ten of the Penna were killed. We should retrieve their weapons. The snowmobiles are also still nearby."

He agreed, and sent some of the men to retrieve the snowmobiles, arms, and supplies of the fallen enemy. Soon, my two throwing axes and sword were back in their sheaths, and my quivers were replenished with arrows.

"At least they have some things of value," Rabbit said, surveying the small mound of armor, weapons, jewelry and coins that had been retrieved from the dead.

A nagging thought flickered in the back of my mind. Slipping aside, I slid out of the encampment and headed toward the open land. Scouting lightly through the shifting landscape, I soon found a good vantage point from which to survey the icy land. A Penna camp stood there, as I had suspected. But it was heavily guarded. They appeared to be building watchtowers, and bands of men were working on them. A glint of light from one of the Penna's helmets caught my attention and I tensed. There were slaves chained hand and foot.

Dropping back down the ridge, I raced back to camp despite my wounded leg.

"Rabbit," I called as soon as I had reached them. "The Penna have set up camp and have gangs of slaves working on it. They are vulnerable and their encampment has no walls. This is the time we should strike."

The Cyan fighters exchanged keen glances. A chance to regain their honor stood upon the open icy land. It was a chance to gain plunder and glory by defeating an entire army. Rabbit nodded slowly and the men grabbed their weapons. We would fight again this night. I steadied my resolve, the love of battle filling me, but the fear threatening to paralyze. I only hoped the love would win over my fear.

5

Three days had passed since the attack. We had successfully captured the Penna's camp, regaining our honor as well as precious resources. I had remained largely out of the fight—completely against my will. Rabbit made it very clear I was not to fight until I had healed. I had protested to no avail, leading him to threaten an actual spanking if I were to disobey. The audacity of the man, to treat me like a child! And yet, he was the commander, and I had no choice but to obey.

With the addition of new men to the Cyan force —when reinforcements arrived—the attitude toward me had changed. Before, I had been tolerated, if not accepted. Now, even the men whose lives I had saved condemned me. Since they despised a fighting Penna woman, I had taken to night patrols, even pitching my tent aside from the rest. Rabbit disliked my withdrawal and ordered me to stay near camp, or once again, another spanking would be in order. The ridiculousness of his sanction tested my resolve to follow any further dictates. He wouldn't dare.

The sun had just set. Cool breezes whispered across the hills of snow. The camp was loud, shattering the natural stillness of the icy land and frightening away the few creatures that still clung to this harsh existence.

I rose, slipping carefully away from my tent. Leaping the low wall, I headed into the frozen hills. In the stillness of the night, I treasured my freedom. The ability to scout and fight without judgment had been taken away, but they could not stop me from scouting and practicing in secret.

After walking fifteen minutes away from camp, I stopped at the top of a large ridge. The surrounding icy land was open to my gaze, nothing moving but snow and wind. I inhaled, stretching slowly. The clear breeze carried just a hint of death. Only the brightest stars were visible, snow from the wind partially obscuring the faintest ones.

Finishing my stretch, I drew my sword and began practicing. Back and forth across the ridge, I thrust and parried, fighting an imaginary opponent. All my skills were gained that way—

shadow fighting. Sometimes an imaginary opponent was harder to fight than a real one. As the moon rose, its glow silvering the snow, I switched weapons.

Doubled axes first. I spun across the ridge, slashing and hacking through imaginary men. First high and then low, defending with one and then with the other. I practiced until my muscles ached. It was my first real exercise since I had been wounded, mostly because Rabbit would not let me out of his sight. I smiled again, nearly laughing. They probably all thought I was daintily asleep like a good little woman.

Sheathing the two throwing axes, I again stretched to ease my muscles and paused before starting my practice with the larger, two-handed axe. The icy land was still, stiller than it had been before. Even the breeze had lightened and was barely stirring the snow.

I drew the two-handed axe and began. I focused on attacking and strength training. The snow dunes were soft enough and didn't dull the axe head too badly when I struck them. So I worked, striking the blade into the snow mounds as if I were cleaving armor.

But it was useless. No matter how I practiced and punished my body, I could not drive the nagging thoughts from my mind—Rabbit and his words on submission. Why was the man looming in my thoughts?

"Why?" I gasped, striking hard at the snowy banks. "Why must a woman submit?" As the question whirled, my anger grew, and so did my strength. I fought the banks until my might gave out and I collapsed, exhausted, upon the sloped side of my latest conquest.

Rolling over, I watched an anthropod scuttling across the ridge. It was hunting, seeking and finding nothing. Its movements were swift as its almost transparent body scurried nearly invisibly across the snow. Suddenly it pounced, drawing out its prey from under a chunk of ice. After pausing, it scurried on, seeking more.

Life on the icy land was like that, I realized. Everyone was always seeking something. Yet when they had found some of what they sought, they could not enjoy it, nor did it satisfy them. Instead, they scuttled on, hurrying through life while trying to find that little bit more before death claimed them. Was that all there was to look forward to in this life? Training, fighting, exhausting oneself, only to rest for a bit before scurrying on to the next encampment, the next battle. Surely there had to be more, something to make all this worthwhile. Something that a woman might find with a man like... No, I was so not going there!

I sighed, preparing to head back to the camp. If I were found outside of it, I feared that Rabbit would punish me—or worse, constantly guard me like a prisoner. He had warned me that I was to limit the use of my leg and to stay nearby. He actually said he would sting my backside with his hand until I never questioned his authority again.

"Alice," came Rabbit's voice, stopping me as I prepared to rise. "Did you think you could slip out of camp without anyone following?" The torch he held in his hand highlighted his masculine features.

Defenses raised, I rose and faced him. "I don't believe it's any of your business if I leave camp or not. I have scouted ahead plenty of times without a problem, and we have no enemies near enough to worry about."

"It is not the Penna that I'm worried about, but your safety in general. The men haven't been around a woman in a very long time. If one of them sees you alone, I think even my warning won't keep them away."

I bristled, anger brimming, then overflowing at Rabbit. "And I suppose you think it is your duty to protect me? And that I'm a weak-willed woman who cannot tell one end of a blade from the other? Perhaps you think I'm helpless too? Even a whore?" I was shaking now, ill-prepared to understand how those I'd fought alongside could now relegate me to the status of helpless burden.

"It is what the men think, not what I think, that matters."

"I care what you believe more than what the men think. You are their commander, after all, and if you ever let me fight again, you are also mine."

"Yes, I am your commander, and yet you disobeyed me." His eyes darkened.

The way he stared caused me to take pause. "I needed to train. I have to work twice as hard to compete with all you arrogant asses."

Rabbit walked toward me so he towered mere inches from my rapidly beating heart. He placed the torch into the snow beside us. "What did I tell you, Alice?"

I swallowed the lump in the back of my throat. "To rest my leg. But my leg is fine, I assure you."

"And?" His stare bored into me.

"To stay near camp."

"What else did I say?"

I raised my head so I stared directly in his eyes. "That you would spank me, sir. But you can't possibly stand by your words."

Rabbit grabbed me firmly by the arm and pulled me down to the snow so I was on all fours. "Yes, I am a man of my word." Before I could even protest, he pulled up my tunic and yanked down the remaining fabric that covered my naked buttocks. "Stay on your hands and knees, or your punishment will be far worse."

I looked over my shoulder in shock. "You can't be serious! You expect me to just allow this?" The snow stung my bare knees, and the light breeze wafted over my damp sex. I was completely exposed to his view, as well as his touch. I knew I would have a fighting chance to resist this spanking if I chose to, but something from deep within held me in position.

He answered with a firm swat to my naked flesh, and then three more before I even knew what was happening. I tried to collapse to my stomach to avoid the spanking. He pulled me back up and said, "You just earned yourself more of a punishment. Stay in position."

I turned my head to stare into his eyes before he swatted me a few more times. The biting sting of his hand caused me to gasp for breath. "Rabbit, please! This has gone far enough!"

"No, my foolish warrior. You will learn that you are not to question my command, my orders, or my concern for your well-being."

Concern for my well-being? It had been quite some time since anyone had cared about me in any way—if ever.

The spanking continued, and I did everything I

could to remain in place. The palms of my hands, my knees, and my ass screamed for mercy. My wounded leg was the least of my discomfort at this time.

Rabbit's palm continued to pepper my backside. Each slap to my exposed bottom brought an alarming desire I couldn't contain. His dominance milked the wetness from my deepest core. I pressed my legs together, desperately hoping he wouldn't see the moisture dripping down my inner thigh. My body rocked forward with each searing swat, causing my nipples to rub against the fabric of my tunic. My body buzzed with life, even as my ass blazed with heat.

"Rabbit! Rabbit, I said stop! That hurts!"

"You are a woman, Alice. A beautiful, exquisite woman." He paused spanking me for a moment, a dead silence in the air. "I admire your strength. I respect your ability to fight. But you are still a woman."

I looked over my shoulder with daggers in my eyes. "So what if I am a woman?" I spat. "Does that mean I should *submit*, as you say? Never!"

Rabbit continued to spank at a quick rate. "Yes, my warrior. Yes!" His hand slapped one cheek and then the next. He covered every inch of skin until tears streamed down my face. He paused the punishment again. "There is nothing wrong with submission, Alice. A strong warrior, and an even stronger woman, would understand that."

Finally, he stopped the assault, stood up fully, and assisted me to a standing position. I quickly adjusted my clothing and stared at the ground. Looking at him now would cause such embarrassment. The act had humiliated me. Not because of the discipline, but because of how it lit my body with a passion I never knew existed.

He tilted my chin with his finger so I had to look into his eyes. "When I give an order, I will trust you will obey it."

"Yes, sir," I whispered.

"I will not hesitate to discipline you again in whatever manner I deem fit."

I nodded, causing Rabbit to drop his hand from my chin.

"You may be able to fight, but you are still an unclaimed woman. You do not belong to a man and, therefore, are vulnerable for the taking. Your safety is my concern."

I collapsed back on the ridge, strength and the will to fight leaving me suddenly. "Then what am I to do? If I remain a soldier, unclaimed, I must be guarded as someone of weakness. What can I do, Rabbit?"

I waited, staring expectantly at him. Seeing that

he had my full attention, Rabbit continued. "Do you wish to be claimed?"

"I wish to fight."

"I see. So you wish to die?"

"I wish to live… fully."

Rabbit paused, finally sitting down alongside me in the snow. Leaning forward, he moved closer to my body, just enough to help ward off the wind that had begun to lift more snow crystals into the air. I lay back, resting against the ridge. The stars were dim now, the light of the moon and the swirling snow flurries nearly eclipsing all the stars, even the wandering ones.

He sighed before speaking with his eyes fixed on the snow mounds ahead. "I've watched you from afar for the last few months, and my respect for you has only increased while being your commander. But I also watch you in battle with a terror I have never known. I fear your death, and I fear losing you." He took a deep breath and added, "I have feelings for you. I see you as more than just a soldier under my command."

I twisted, staring at Rabbit in disbelief, light from the moon casting haunting shadows around us. I had been taught that adoration was rarely found among the ones who died by blade. Doing so could lead to your own death. You fought for your own life and only concerned yourself with surviving the battle.

Rabbit continued. "I don't know if there is a Penna way of doing things, and I don't want to insult you. But I would like to make you mine. I want you, Alice."

I spoke, my voice shaking, and his close proximity did nothing to dispel the pounding within my chest. "I am no longer a Penna. My family is dead." I paused and tried to find the right words, but the awkwardness of the conversation made my insides quiver. "What do you mean by 'mine'?"

"The Cyan believe in claiming a woman first, and then ultimately finalizing that claim by uniting in marriage. Do the Penna marry?"

I shook my head. "No. Not anymore. That belief is considered archaic."

Rabbit laughed. "Archaic to commit for life?"

I smiled, grateful that the awkward air seemed to be lifting a little. "Yes, extremely archaic. The Penna believe in science, and black and white facts. Emotions do not belong anywhere in the equation. Love is not something that adds value to progression. The only reason a man and woman unite is for the purpose of breeding. To continue the Penna line. You don't need marriage for that to occur."

"So no one loves each other?" Rabbit looked shocked by this information.

"No. What purpose does that serve?"

"Is there no pleasure allowed?"

I shrugged. "I assume pleasure occurs during the breeding process, but love does not."

"That's a shame," Rabbit said in a soft voice. "Another reason I am happy you are no longer a Penna. I would like to someday give you pleasure and love."

"You would?" I wasn't sure how to respond or act to Rabbit's words. They were so direct—just like him—and they were so true and honest. I felt I owed him the same in return.

"I would like that as well," I said in not much more than a whisper.

"I respect you as a fierce warrior. Because of that respect, I will not force you into marriage. This will be your choice. But I would like you to at least be open to the idea. It is the way of the Cyan." He turned to face me fully, the intensity of his look highlighted by the moonlight. "But I do not want you to be forced into any match, Alice, even with me."

With the intensity of his gaze, and the way my name rolled gently off his lips, I could well believe that he cared for me. A tingle flickered through me. Could I care for him enough to forsake a belief that was ingrained in me since birth, one that danced through my veins?

I spoke in a rush. "I respect you, Rabbit, more than I have ever respected any man. But..." I paused, looking away into the icy night and then back to him again. This time I looked at him not as a commander, but as a man.

I studied his profile. His black hair was silvered at the temples, and his beard was stark black against his dark skin. By my reckoning, he was no longer young, but not yet old. His jaw was firm and set, showing the determination that had enabled him to lead a band of soldiers. His eyes, however, stopped me. Respect and caring lingered in their depths; no judgment lay hidden there, and no scorn. The slight twitch of his eye, accentuated by the moonlight, betrayed the worry he felt at my pause.

Drawing a deep breath, I finished what I had to say. "I see in your eyes that you do not look at me as do the other men. The other men look upon me as a conquest, something to boast of in the long evening hours. In your eyes, I see respect mingled with longing. My heart is hard. It cannot yet give love. Yet, perhaps I could say the four words you said to me. The words: I care for you."

"So you have agreed to be mine?"

I nodded, staring directly into his eyes. "Yes."

Rabbit smiled, his face lighting up with the relief my words brought. He reached out and grabbed my hand.

"Give me time, and give me the freedom to fight," I added.

He nodded, still smiling before glancing at the sky. His smile turned to a frown, and I too glanced to the heavens. The moon had almost set, and the icy land was plunging into thick blackness. The last stars that had blazed bright in the indigo vault had disappeared. I looked at Rabbit, alarm tingling through me.

"The clouds are coming in." I paused, glancing around the horizon.

"It's a blizzard," he finished. "We must run for camp, now."

Without hesitation, we ran hand in hand. When I stumbled, Rabbit pulled me back to my feet and our hands never left each other's grasp. Despite the desperateness of the situation, I felt exhilarated as we ran. We made good time, leaping over the snowdrifts, and sliding or skidding down the steeper ones. But the storm was faster.

Wind whipped around us, scattering dozens of snowy granules like miniature sling stones that stung any exposed skin. The roar of the wind increased, and just as it was upon us, the wall of the encampment appeared. Kicking our speed up to a full sprint, we jointly vaulted the wall and dropped into shelter behind it.

We crouched behind the shelter. The snowstorm whirled around us, pelting the wall and every inch of exposed skin with snow and ice. Tugging on my hand, Rabbit half led and half dragged me down the wall of ice.

Visibility was down, I could not even see Rabbit's torso, only his disembodied hand and arm. Suddenly he yanked me forward, and I stumbled into a tent as he pulled the flaps shut.

"We lucked out," he said, glancing around. "At least we hit your tent and not one of the other men's."

The snow beat against the door, but I was grateful it no longer pummeled against my body.

"Yes." I nodded. "The storm came on fast." Heading for the mattress of my bed, the only seat in the tent, I stumbled and nearly fell. My right, injured, leg could no longer bear my weight.

Concern etched Rabbit's brow. "Are you all right? Did your wound break open again?"

Collapsing in a seated position, I lifted up the edge of my ice-encrusted tunic, and pulled up my pants. The bandage was red with blood and thickly coated with snow.

I nodded with a grimace. "It looks like it broke open. Either from trying to defeat snow drifts with a sword, or from trying to outrun the storm."

"Or from a combination of the two," he replied, moving to the side of the tent and fetching the medical supplies, and some of the water that had been placed there when my wound was originally cared for.

I watched his every move. He looked different. I saw a man who had declared he wanted me. I saw a man who took me in hand and soundly spanked my bottom with no clothing separating his hand from my flesh. I saw a man I respected. Was this a man I could also call mine?

"We cannot let this get infected. I hope you trust my hand." He smirked. "It can do more than just deliver punishment to a well-deserving behind."

I did everything to conceal the smile that threatened to wash over my face. "I can scarcely think of a man I would trust to treat my injuries other than you." I glanced around. The plain, black-walled tent had been my home since I'd joined the Cyan army. Tonight the walls were lightened by powdered white, and the whistling wind buffeting the taut fabric. "I would prefer your hand doing this, rather than peppering my backside," I said as Rabbit prepared the wound wash with warm water and various herbs. "Though I believe the sting to be the same."

He smiled and turned to face me with a mischievous look in his eye. "Yes. My hand is a master of the sting."

I turned, pulling the pants away from my leg just enough to permit access to the wound. Rabbit squatted before me and carefully unwrapped the bandages.

The wound was inflamed and hot, with pus oozing around the edges. I winced, and Rabbit looked grim. With a degree of care and gentleness that surprised me, he washed the wound. Over and over he washed it, until no trace of pus or dried blood remained visible. His touch was gentle. His skill was also clear as he effortlessly mixed, pounded, and otherwise prepared herbs to place on the wound. After the herbs were prepared, he stepped back and fetched a flask from the medicine chest.

"This will burn but it should prevent infection from setting in again."

I raised my eyebrows and then gasped as he poured the liquid over the wound. Stinging pain stole my breath. As soon as he finished pouring, he smeared the herbal preparation over the injury. The herbs soothed the sting, enabling me to catch my breath again.

"That may clean the wound, but it hurts," I exclaimed, watching as he began bandaging the injury.

He applied a layer of absorbent cotton. Then he wrapped a narrow bandage of linen over it to hold the cotton in place.

"The linen will help prevent contamination of the wound, and the cotton can be changed to prevent infection from increasing. The herbal preparation will remain good for some days, even in these conditions, and you can change and redress the wound nightly. That will also help keep infection away."

I nodded, wincing as he began cleaning the cut on my face with some of the liquid.

"Is that really necessary? Just because the wound is smaller doesn't mean it stings less."

"It probably stings more. But if you don't sit still, I will make your bottom sting as well." Rabbit smiled. "Keeping down infection and keeping the wound clean will decrease the severity of the scarring and speed healing."

His breath was on my face. The close proximity made me nervous as he applied some of the herbal salve to the injury. When his hand dropped, he brushed it gently along my jaw. Then he walked back to the chest to put away the things he had used. Reaching up, I brushed my fingers gently over the wound and let my hand linger along my jaw, relishing his touch.

"It seems strange," I said, relaxing and letting down my guard at Rabbit's care and gentleness. "I do not feel I have to prove my strength to you right now, yet I worry you'll find me weak."

He shook his head and said, "That is where you are wrong, my fighter. When you don't feel the need to prove your strength, it is then that I see your true power."

"It always seemed hard to me, that when the men were trained to use the sword, women were simply told how to die on one," I said, glancing down at my hands. The snowstorm continued to rage around us, providing the only sound in the silence.

Rabbit broke the silence after a few moments. "Although I hate the sense of fear I feel seeing you fight, I prefer it to you not knowing how. I know you can kill with the same ruthless nature as I."

I turned, watching Rabbit carefully. "Ruthless nature? Is that said with liking or disgust?"

He sighed, slipping closer to me. He stretched out his arm, and slid it behind my shoulders. Leaning sideways, I rested against his shoulder. A strange feeling of protection and comfort stole over me.

"It is said as fact. I have no disgust towards you," he whispered. "Quite the opposite."

"You are different than the men I have known," I said, glancing at his face, profiled sharply against the black tent. "They treat me as less than the dirty snow on the bottom of their boots, yet it seems you see me as more."

He nodded. "I do. I see you as a fellow fighter. I want you in battle right beside me." He moved in ever so slightly, so I could feel his breath against my lips. "I also see a woman I would very much like to be inside of. I see a woman I would like to be with in all ways."

"I would like that too," I admitted. My heart soared unexpectedly at the prospect of fighting alongside this man whom I now respected. But my body throbbed with need at his proposal of intimacy. "It would be my pleasure to fight at your side until death parts us," I said, my voice barely above a whisper.

He leaned in completely and kissed me softly. This was not a kiss of force, or aggression, or even sexual need. This kiss was gentler than a light, chilled breeze—but had the power of a whiteout storm.

My breath caught and I wrapped my arms around his neck, kissing him back with complete freedom. I felt safe with Rabbit; protected, but at the same time valued for the powerful woman I was.

He broke the kiss, but only pulled away mere inches from my face. "And what about my other desires?"

I knew he wanted more. In truth, I too wanted more.

I blushed. "I don't have an answer for that... yet." I gave the answer I felt I *should* give, even though my rebel soul wanted to be taken by his need.

Rabbit leaned forward, brushing his lips gently along my hairline. "Then we had better part ways tonight, since I don't trust my wants and desires. We have a long journey back to my home village tomorrow. The Mad Hatter, the Cyan general, is meeting us there with more reinforcements. Our army is beaten down and we need to rest and rebuild." Rising softly, he went to the door of the tent. "Sleep well, my dark feather." He exited without another word, the only sounds being the swirling snow and biting wind.

6

We had finally reached and settled in to the village of Danis. Our travels were on hold until reinforcements arrived and the injured could heal. Camp was set up for the soldiers for housing so we could also continue to train. But for the time being, we were all taking this time to lick our wounds while Rabbit met with The Mad Hatter to decide what the Cyans' next move would be. We were at a standstill, and rather than the break and rest giving me comfort, as I'm sure it did for many, I felt a constant sense of unease and anxiety.

I stretched out on my mattress and pulled my arms behind my head, taking in the thick, clean smell of freshly fallen snow. I closed my eyes and stared up at the plain ceiling of my new living quarters. When I tried to turn onto my side, I winced. I still suffered slightly from the wound I had taken to the leg, but it was quickly healing, and I expected to be fully recovered in a few days.

I took in another breath and glanced out the small window of my hut, staring at the night sky. At this location in the icy land, the stars were clearly visible at night, and this was something I enjoyed. I loved to watch the stars, but I didn't love sleeping in this kind of hut.

But then again, it was a hut that all soldiers had to sleep in. As part of Cyan's army, I was required to sleep in the same location as all the other men. Higher ranking soldiers were assigned to a sleeping unit that was big enough to hold a sleeping mat, a small table, and had enough room to walk around. Others were assigned to group huts big enough to sleep several. Being the only female, I had my own. But I missed the simple tents we used when we went off to battle. The huts surrounding Rabbit's home in Danis seemed permanent, and permanence scared me. I preferred the freedom of the open icy land and the ability to pick up at a moment's notice.

I would rather ride around the icy land at night on a snowmobile instead of being confined to a living space. I wasn't born to spend my nights in a small sleeping hut. I was born to roam Wonderland and explore all there was to explore. Sleep never came easy, for my mind stayed busy no matter how exhausted I was.

I turned onto my back after wincing again. I took in another deep breath and gathered saliva in my mouth before spitting it out. After spending so much time out in the icy land, I had become accustomed to the feeling of snow and grit in my teeth. At first, that had bothered me, but now it was almost something I bypassed every day. I just learned to spit it out and deal with it.

The soldier in the next sleeping hut over groaned, the sound easily relaying the pain he was in. He had suffered a great leg wound in the last battle. The battle that had wiped out nearly half of Rabbit's army. I blinked and shuddered at the thought of all who had died. The only saving grace was the last battle was won. Honor had been regained. And as much as I hated to admit it, we'd had no choice but to head back to Danis, where Rabbit resided, to build up our forces, heal, and prepare for another war.

Even though I was hardly haunted by my past fights, this past battle stuck with me, and even gave me nightmares. Fighting against a side that was once mine, ate at my soul. I was an expert archer, but the last fight had tested my strength, my mental capacity, and my bravery. While I had made it out alive, half of the army had not.

Now that the battle was over, the courtyard where the army slept seemed much quieter than usual. Everything seemed motionless as everyone was still in a mourning state for the fellow fighters lost. The man in the hut on my other side had succumbed to his wounds from the battle, and even though he had snored like a pig and kept me up at night, I found myself willing to do anything to hear that snore again.

A rustling sound startled me, and I bolted up into a sitting position, my senses heightened. I sat there in the dark, staring in the direction of the entrance to my hut. Through the small slit at the bottom of the cloth door, I saw slight shadows caused by the light of a candle, and carefully got to my feet.

Without making a sound, I moved to the other side of the hut and retrieved my small knife, sharp and gleaming in the moonlight. By now, I had trained long enough to not cower in the face of danger, no matter how large and terrifying it was. Even if this danger was enough to kill me, backing down from a fight would never be an option.

Swallowing a mouthful of grit and courage, I took a step forward, my blade in front of me.

Then the cloth door disappeared in the blink of

an eye, and a rider on a snowmobile drove to the entrance. The rider held a lantern high above his head. All I could see was the shadow of the rider and my heart rate spiked, sending shudders throughout my body. We had just defeated the enemy. The last thing I wanted was to fight again.

"Remain calm, Alice," came a soothing, deep voice.

I immediately dropped the blade that I'd readied for attack and let out a sigh. "What the hell do you think you were doing, storming into my doorway on a snowmobile? I almost killed you," I said stiffly, bending to retrieve my knife, automatically cleaning dirt from the blade. I slipped the blade back into its sheath and turned back to face the soldier. "What is the meaning of this midnight meeting? Are we off to battle again after we just fought?"

The soldier, still clad in his battle tunic, slid off his snowmobile and paced into my hut, drawing the cloth door shut. Shaking his head, he placed the lantern on the ground and dug in his satchel for a scroll wrapped together with a silky red ribbon.

"This is for you," the soldier said, handing me the rolled paper.

I stared at him and felt a lump form in the back of my dry throat. "Who is this from?"

"Rabbit," the soldier said, placing the scroll in my hands.

I stared at him for a long moment.

"I would suggest opening it, as it requires an urgent and immediate response," the soldier prompted, gesturing to the scroll.

I let out a soft sigh but removed the ribbon. Before I opened the letter, however, I reveled in the touch of fine satin. Then I unrolled the scroll and read through the black script. It was clearly a formal production, as the font of the text was smooth and sleek, nothing like a typical man's handwriting.

"What is this?" I demanded.

"It is an invitation to his home," the soldier told me curtly. "He requires your presence in his home for a dinner in celebration of our recent victory. I require your response right away, since the dinner is tomorrow night."

I looked up at him through narrowed eyes and handed back the invitation. "What if I would rather not go? What if I would rather stay and train?" I said the words, but my heart fluttered at the thought of seeing Rabbit again. The journey back to Danis had taken days, and I had seen very little of him during it. I had actually felt physical pain in my heart at times, thinking that he may have returned to the arms of another woman who was doing a fine job keeping him company and rewarding him for his bravery and servitude to the Cyan army. The thought of him being with another made me ill, and I hated that he could control my thoughts and emotions so easily, not even being present to do so.

The soldier smiled wryly at me. "I'm sorry. Your attendance is mandatory."

"Then why have I received an invitation?" I demanded. "If it is an invitation, I should be allowed to decline it if I wish." I wasn't sure why I was putting up such a resistance. I wasn't one for playing silly games, and the truth of the matter was that I truly wanted to attend.

"It's with Commander White," the soldier told me. "It would be wise not to deny an invitation to his home. After all, you are a soldier in his army, and you are under his command."

I swallowed back any further retort, not missing the fact that this time, he'd used Rabbit's formal title. "Fine. I will attend."

"Thank you for the good news," he replied. "A servant from his house will be by to pick you up tomorrow afternoon."

Servant? It seemed odd that Rabbit would have a servant. I had only known him as a commander of an army, who slept on cots and ate from tin bowls. The picture of him living as a man of wealth seemed foreign. And why would I need to be picked up so early? What would I do during all that time before the celebration?

"I thought it was a dinner? Doesn't that mean eating after the sun has gone down?" I asked, blinking in confusion.

"Yes, but Rabbit would rather you look more like a woman," he replied flatly. "Upon your arrival, servants will take you to get cleaned and properly dressed for the dinner." The soldier looked at me from head to toe. "A bath would do you good."

I let out a long sigh. "I will await the servant." I did my best to smile.

"Very well," the soldier told me, taking a step back towards the door. "Remember that a servant will be around to your quarters later tomorrow afternoon. Be prepared."

"I am always prepared," I told him smugly.

All he did was nod, then he swiftly left my tent, jumping onto his snowmobile, spun it expertly in a tight circle, and disappeared into the night.

I took another deep breath and let myself relax on my mattress. Again, I stared up at the ceiling and listened to the sounds of the night, somewhat in disbelief of Rabbit.

Rabbit was the commander of this army.

During my stay, I had learned plenty. He was the cousin of The Mad Hatter. Rabbit was in training to be the next general, as he was deemed the next to follow The Mad Hatter. He had a hand in the training of the soldiers for the most recent battles, and his reputation as a fair, but tough, leader blanketed the camp. Word had spread swiftly about me being 'claimed' by him. No one spoke of it, but all kept their distance. Vulgar comments had completely ceased.

I shut my eyes, feeling a bit of sleepy crust nestle in the corners. My thoughts drifted to his discipline and his talk about the need for submission. The stinging correction to my backside had been unlike any sensation I had experienced. Ever since the last spanking, I could only wonder if it would happen again. If I did indeed marry this man, would I find my buttocks constantly warmed? As appalled as I should have been by his display of overbearing masculinity, I couldn't for the life of me forget the feeling. And if I truly were being honest, I craved it again.

Since that moment, Rabbit had been frequently on my mind. Even in the midst of battle, he had been on my mind. His skin was the smoothest I had seen, and it was a rich color, darker than the men of the Penna. Though he had scars, and though his appearance revealed an ice age worn warrior, he also had an allure.

I shook my head and took another deep breath. But even as I nestled down and drifted off into sleep, I found myself thinking of Rabbit in every way possible.

7

I hardly slept, which wasn't something new for me. The idea of going to bed, closing your eyes, and waking up with the sun was a luxury not granted to a soldier. We were trained to always be ready, and that was a habit I couldn't break even if we were supposed to be resting and recovering. I woke early, just as the sun was rising above the horizon, painting the sky with pinks and yellows and reds. I enjoyed being out in the early morning, before everyone woke and disrupted the tranquility of the day.

I headed out of my hut early that morning with the intention to train. Even though we were ordered to rest and recover, I still felt the need to keep up my physical stamina. I trekked out to the short training area in the middle of the living quarters. The living quarters were a cluster of huts where all the soldiers slept, and the tents surrounded a communal training plain that held a variety of weapons which allowed soldiers to hone their skills. I was the only fighter who visited the training area every day and seemed to stay there for hours, even though my body begged me to stop.

Just like every other day, I made it to the training center and dug my feet in the snow to ground myself. I had taken my personal sword with me and now pulled it from the sheath that was slung over my shoulders. With a calm breath, I watched the early morning sun glint off the blade. I launched into a rigorous training session, wielding my blade expertly. As the sun started to rise, more soldiers awoke to see me already at work.

As soon as the sun stood overhead, I stopped and let my body rest for a moment. I sat down on the freezing snow, breathing heavily. My mouth was incredibly dry and sweat poured down my forehead, soaking my uniform. Hearing the crunch of snow, I turned to my right to see Cheshire standing a few feet away.

"What do you want?" I asked as I stood, ready to fight if that was his plan.

"I'm simply watching the great Penna warrior in action," he said with a smirk.

I swiped at a long lock of hair that hung loose

in my face. "Why do you hate me so much? Is it just because I'm a Penna? Or is it because I am a woman and a better soldier than you can be any day?"

Cheshire crossed his arms against his chest and laughed loudly. "That really is funny. I could squash you, little girl. I wouldn't even break a sweat doing so."

"Then why don't you try? What holds you back?" I taunted. It was true that Cheshire could crush me in a hand-to-hand battle, but I would damn sure put up a fight.

"Well, for one, Rabbit has ordered all hands off you. And as much as I would love to teach you a lesson, I do follow my commander's orders. Plus, Rabbit happens to be a good friend of mine. So even though I think he's lost his mind keeping you around, I respect his decision." He shifted his weight from one foot to the next while he sized me up from head to toe. "And second, I like watching you. You fascinate me."

"What?" I snapped. "What the hell do you mean; *I fascinate you*?"

"So tell me. How did you get those feathers?" he asked, glancing at my exposed wrist.

I could have told him to go fuck himself and leave me alone, but why bother? He wouldn't leave, and I had nothing to hide. Plus, knowing Cheshire, he would probably like knowing he was upsetting me. I wouldn't give him the satisfaction. "I was injected with cDermo-1 as a child and they grew over time."

"Do they really keep you warm?" Cheshire seemed genuine in his question, nor did I pick up on any hate or judgment.

"They do. I think that the chemicals in my bloodstream keep me warmer than the actual feathers do. It's not like feathers cover my entire body."

"Do they hurt? Or can you feel them in your skin?"

"No. They feel the same as the hair on your head. It hurt when I tried to pluck one out to see if the feather would grow back." The memory of how I'd hoped I could pluck them out of me and be free of the deformity forever filled me with a renewed shame of what I hated so very much.

"And did it? Grow back?" Cheshire actually seemed nice—even likeable.

"It grew back," I mumbled as I looked down at my feet.

"You're lucky to have them."

"I don't think so."

"But you are. You have no idea the cold that we feel." He kicked a pile of snow in front of him. "My toes ache from several cases of frostbite, my bones creak when I bend because surely I have frozen every part of my body at some point in my life. I am never truly warm. I live a life of constant cold, and my only hope is to make it tolerable with the layers of clothing I wear. I hate you fucking Penna for so many reasons, but I will give your kind one bit of credit. You were smart with the feathers. Other Cyans may not agree with me, but I would take an injection of that dermo crap you just described any day over the freezing cold I have to endure."

"I've never considered myself lucky," I admitted.

"Well, you are. You are alive, aren't you?"

"If you think the feathers are so great, then why do you call me a mutant?" I asked.

"Because I can." He gave a small smirk—or was it a smile? And with that last statement, Cheshire turned on his heels and left me standing alone in the snow.

Confused at first by Cheshire's visit, I eventually smiled when I realized that surprise exchange was his rough attempt at trying to make peace. It wasn't exactly friendly, but it most certainly wasn't hostile. I realized then, that that was the way Cheshire was. Gruff. But regardless of how he said it, or how he acted, that was most definitely his awkward effort to connect with me.

"Alice?" a voice I did not recognize from behind questioned.

Startled, I jumped to my feet, grabbing my sword. When I turned around with the blade, I saw what I assumed to be one of Rabbit's servants staring at me. The servant, a young girl, paled when she saw the sharp blade pointed directly at her throat.

"I did not mean you any harm!" she claimed, taking a step back.

I let out the breath I had been holding and tucked the blade back into the sheath on my back. "My apologies."

The girl looked surprised that I had softened so easily.

"I-I am here to pick you up for the celebration dinner tonight," the servant said quietly, still seeming a little frightened of my blade.

I nodded and wiped a bead of sweat from my face. "Where are we going?"

She calmed down a little and looked more at ease. "We are going to Rabbit's home, where I and a few other servants will help prepare you for the dinner."

I nodded again and left the training area with her. As I walked, I kept my distance from the servant who was so prim and proper in her female attire. While I wore blood-stained, loose fighting clothes, she was draped in thick layers of elegant cloth in vibrant colors.

"What do you guys plan on doing to me once I reach Rabbit's home?" I questioned as we slowly left the training center.

"You will have a team of his attendants who will tend to your needs," the girl said. "We will help you bathe, dress, and paint yourself so you will look acceptable for the dinner."

I silently nodded in acceptance, though her words seemed totally foreign to me.

After about twenty minutes of walking in a light snowstorm, the house appeared in my view and I almost stopped in my tracks. It had been a while since I had seen a house of such grandeur.

"The house is made up of three main parts," the girl explained. "There is the main building, which houses the large dining hall and several small meeting areas. There is the bedroom wing, which molds in a U-shape around the main building and contains several lavish bedrooms. The final area is the courtyard, which is sectioned off by stone walls and allows members of the household to enjoy themselves outside while never actually leaving the protection of the grounds."

Every building in the grounds appeared to be made with the purest stone, which was of a rich, snowy color. It was strong enough to keep out anything or anyone, and reflected the light of the sun, causing it to almost glimmer during the daytime. Intricate carvings were made into some of the stones, displaying detailed patterns and shapes.

"Is everything all right?" the girl asked, noticing my surprise.

I blinked and nodded, catching up to her. "Everything is just fine. The house seems a little larger than I expected."

The young servant smiled softly as we approached the gates to the courtyard, where several guards were waiting for us.

"Yes, it does have that effect, doesn't it?" the girl said as we approached the guards. Facing them, she said, "I have Alice, an invitee of Rabbit's. She'll attend the celebration dinner as a guest, and she'll receive honors for contributing to our latest victories."

The guards nodded and allowed us into the courtyard. My brows furrowed together tightly and I gripped the servant by the shoulder. When she winced a little, I dropped my hand. Sometimes I hardly remembered how strong a grip I had.

"I am receiving honors tonight?" I asked in confusion.

The girl rubbed her shoulder and nodded. "Yes. Rabbit has deemed you a great asset to our army and has named you as one of the reasons why we have achieved victory. You will receive honors before The Mad Hatter himself."

The courtyard was massive, housing hundreds of small benches and community settings. Several people wandered around, talking amongst themselves. When the servant and I passed, the conversations dropped and everyone seemed to look at me.

While I was usually proud, and held my head high, I now felt a little out of place as everyone could clearly see my difference, and take note that I was obviously a woman in men's clothing. I could also see they were all trying to see my feathers for themselves. Luckily, they were mostly concealed, and you would have to be up close to see them.

I followed the servant down the polished stone pathway that cut through the courtyard. I could tell that the girl was still a little upset about my strong grip, and I didn't bother to apologize for it. I had killed many men without asking for forgiveness, so merely causing a little ache in someone's shoulder hardly put a tick on my conscience.

I kept close behind her as we started up the grand steps, which were polished and of the same snowy color as the bricks. Each step contained intricate carvings and I got caught up in studying one of them.

"Alice!" the servant snapped, already at the top of the staircase. "Come now. We need to hurry."

I abandoned the artwork and hurried up to the top of the stairs where the girl was waiting. A pair of guards stood at the wide double doors which were decorated in paintings. Like before, I paused to stare at them, and the servant had to physically pull me away. Or, at least, she tried.

I had a precise sense of balance and strength, so when the girl tried to pull me away from the doors, I did not budge. After a few moments, I voluntarily walked away from the doors and followed her down one of the many halls.

The inside of the main building was just as intricate as the outside. Several tapestries hung down the walls, along with hundreds of different paintings, some of the landscape, and others of heroes in war.

The floor was highly polished, and it amazed me that it was possible to almost clearly see my reflection in it. It was as if I were walking on a block of ice. I stopped to stare down at myself and realized that other people probably thought I was a wanderer, instead of a soldier in the army, judging by the way I looked.

I quickly hastened to follow the servant down the hallway, pausing before a set of polished doors similar to the ones on the front of the main building.

"You will be bathed, clothed, and made up before tonight's celebratory dinner in four hours," the girl said as she heaved open the door.

"I have four hours to get dressed? Why would I need four hours?" I asked.

"You need to look at yourself in a mirror. That would answer your question," she told me with a subtle smirk.

I restrained the urge to punch the female in the face and merely followed her into the dressing room, where a team of attendants sat waiting for my arrival. All of them were dressed in heavy layers of silks and satins, makeup perfectly applied to their faces. I felt as though I was looking at a set of porcelain dolls.

"Hello, Alice," said a second servant as she got to her feet. "We are so lucky to have you in attendance. We cannot wait to help transform you." The sweetness was so thick, I almost wished to be standing beside Cheshire and the other assholes outside.

I groaned inwardly and looked back at the first servant, who was busy shutting the doors. Running the back of my hand across my forehead, thankful that I was out of the sun, I could feel my sweat drying into my uniform, making the cloth stiff and hard to move in.

"We have already drawn up a bath of essential oils for you," one of the servants said as she opened the doors to a luxurious bathroom.

Like the rest of the house, the bathroom had high ceilings and was adorned with beautiful paintings. At the center of the room was a large tub filled with some kind of purple substance that was heavily scented. Another, smaller tub stood off in the corner, filled with water. I wrinkled my nose.

"Now, if you will hand us your battle-worn wardrobe, we would be happy to help you bathe," one of the servants told me, already reaching for the sleeve of my shirt.

Instinctively, I reached out and grabbed her wrist. Seeing the startled look on her face, I dropped her wrist with an apologetic expression.

"I'm sorry," I said quietly. "I am a warrior, and once a Penna. I have been taught to be alert and to watch myself."

The servant nodded in understanding, but she still seemed a tad frightened. "Can... can you get your feathers wet?" she asked, clearly afraid of my answer.

"Yes," I simply answered.

"If you would like," another servant jumped in, "we can let you undress in private and you can bathe in the oils of your own accord. If you would like to, there is also a tub of water to bathe in to cleanse yourself of dirt."

I nodded. "That sounds wonderful. Thank you."

With that, I walked into the bathroom and pushed the doors shut. Sighing, I stripped off my uniform, finally glad to be out of it. My naked body was covered from head to toe in grime. A thick air of musk exuded from my body, and I suddenly felt extremely unclean. Usually, I was used to all that came with weeks of not fully bathing, but now that I was in Rabbit's home, I felt incredibly dirty and impure.

I let my dark hair flow down past my shoulders. I was so used to putting it up in a band that it felt foreign to have it flow down my back. It was dirty and matted with blood, sweat, and icy particles.

I padded across the bathroom and gently slid into the tub filled with water. Compared to the cold water I usually bathed in, this was a blessing. It was warm and pure, easy on my skin. I let my entire body soak under the water for a few moments before getting to work on my filth.

For the next twenty minutes, I scrubbed off all the dirt from my body, which irritated my skin and made it incredibly pink. But I was just happy to be rid of all the filth. Looking down at the feathers on my wrists and then my ankles, I found my mindset shifting. I knew that only a short while earlier, I would have wished that I could just scrub those off as easily as I could scrub off my stink. I had never given much thought to my feathers until I left the Penna, only to be called a mutant by Cheshire when I joined the Cyan. The feathers had made me even more different, and that had shamed me. I had hated them so much. But now, after Cheshire's admission that he actually envied me for their ability to keep me warm, I felt differently. He was right. I had never felt the bite of cold so bitter that every cell in my body would ache. Perhaps they weren't as awful as I'd once believed.

Finally, I rose from the water and quickly ran across the bathroom to the other tub, which was filled with that purple, thick liquid. I dipped one finger in it and drew it across the surface, noting that it was thick and syrupy. Taking a deep breath, I slowly dipped one foot in, followed by the other. I let my body sink into the oil.

While the water of the first bath was clear and easy to move around in, the oil in the second one was thick, and it felt like I was trapped in quicksand. I was almost startled for a moment, but then I reminded myself that I was in Rabbit's house, not out in the icy battlefield.

I let the oils sink into every crevice of my body,

and the scent overwhelmed my senses. The aroma was almost fruity, almost floral, but I couldn't tell exactly what combination it was. It was a blessing compared to the rough soaps I and the other soldiers used while washing in the communal bathing areas.

I tipped my head back and rested it on the back of the tub, staring up at the ceiling. Before I knew it, my eyes were shut. I hadn't realized how tired I was, and it was easy for me to slip into a gentle, light sleep. As I was always alert for enemies, I was used to sleeping in a light state, just in case I had to be on the move at a moment's notice.

Just as I was sinking into a deeper sleep, I was jolted awake by the servants, who were all crowded around the bathtub. I jumped, my heart starting.

"We thought something had happened to you, Alice," one of the servants squeaked. "Please, forgive us for disturbing you."

I shook my head to clear myself from my small nap, and rose from the tub, my body dripping with the thick oils.

"It's all right," I mumbled as one of the servants handed me a thick, soft towel.

I wrapped the towel around my shoulders and reveled in how soft it was to the touch as the servants filed out, stepping back into the bedroom.

The wardrobe, which was made of thick, dark wood, was open, revealing a set of clothes.

I stopped in the bathroom doorway.

"Is there something wrong?" one of the servants asked me.

"Do I have to get dressed up?" I asked.

Another servant nodded. "As you will receive honors from The Mad Hatter this evening, it would be proper to dress in the right attire."

I drew the towel tighter around my body and walked forward. The cool stone floor was slick under my feet, smooth compared to the packed snow of the icy land.

"This is what we have for you to wear to the celebratory dinner," a girl said as she removed a long, crimson gown from the wardrobe.

The gown was a deep red color that briefly reminded me of blood. It was garnished with crystals and other jewels, and it seemed to flow effortlessly. It was a one-shouldered dress, with beading on the shoulder strap.

"You want me to actually wear this?" I questioned. All of the servants nodded with smiles. "My feathers will show."

"That doesn't matter," one girl said. "It's no secret you are a Penna. We don't need to hide that fact. If anything, it fascinates us all."

"Once you have finished drying yourself off,"

another servant said, "we'll help you into the gown."

I nodded and quickly dried off my body. I stood still as the servants helped me into the crimson gown, and I suddenly felt like a different person.

No longer did I feel like the warrior who had slain one hundred men. No longer did I feel like the only woman in the army. No longer did I feel huge, bulky, and powerful.

I smiled. So, this was what it was to feel like a woman. I felt as elegant as the servants in this gown, and felt like I belonged with the rest of the females in the house. I felt beautiful, classy, cleansed.

"Now we will help you with your hair and your face," a servant said. She reached out to touch my hand, but another girl shook her head in warning.

Instead, I followed all of the servants into the bathroom again, where I sat down on a plush dressing chair. Before me on the counter stood hundreds of small glass bottles and discs, all filled with different colors, with all the lost colors of Wonderland, it seemed.

A servant grabbed a thick hairbrush from the counter and carefully raised it above my head. In the floor-to-ceiling mirror, she met my eyes and we shared a confirmation.

She stroked the brush through my long hair,

pulling out all the knots and drying it. I winced a few times when my hair was pulled, but I sat through it. Next, I sat through the servant winding my hair up into an elegant updo, finished by clipping it together with a jeweled clasp that matched my crimson gown.

"Do you like your hair?" the servant asked, and that was when I realized that I had shut my eyes in the process.

I opened them again to see how beautiful my dark hair was. It had a certain shine to it and was piled on top of my head in an elegant, sophisticated manner. It seemed so different from the usual messy pile I threw it in when I trained or went to battle.

"It looks fine," I said flatly. A lump formed in my throat, and I found it incredibly difficult to swallow.

One of the servants grabbed one of the glasses in front of me on the counter and opened it, smoothing a little red onto her finger. Immediately, I thought it was blood, but it was only some kind of powder.

"Now, please close your eyes," she said, and I did so. The servant smoothed the bit of red powder over the tops of my eyelids and it was a strange sensation to feel.

After the servant finished, I opened my eyes

and jumped a little. Seeing red at the tops of my eyes startled me, but I had to remind myself that I was not wounded. It was only a little makeup, used to enhance my beauty.

I sat through a few more minutes of beauty prepping as the servants added color to my cheeks and lips, the paint making them appear darker and more vibrant. Soon, I looked like the servants: polished, painted, and porcelain.

"Your shoes," one of the servants said as she came back into the bathroom.

She held out a pair of crimson slippers to match the gown I was wearing. The slippers were soft to the touch and fit well on my feet, glimmering with the jewels in the light.

"Now all we need is jewelry," another servant said. She asked me if I felt comfortable wearing jewelry.

I stared flatly at my reflection. "I have never worn jewels in my entire life. I don't know what it feels like to be adorned with them at all."

The servant merely stared at me before leaving the room and coming back with a heavy wooden chest. She set it on the counter and opened it, revealing a mess of jewels that were strung on a chain. The servant rifled through them for a few moments before pulling out a string of red rubies.

I sat still as she strung the gems around my

neck and clasped it at the back. The necklace was heavy and pressed down against my sternum, but it was no heavier than the armor I once wore. I had lifted grown men onto my back and carried them through miles in the freezing temperatures during the most recent battle. I could most certainly handle a dainty necklace.

"You are all ready, Alice," the first servant announced, inviting me to stand up.

"This is it?" I asked as I stood and glanced once more in the mirror. I stared at a stranger. A beautiful, dainty, elegant stranger. Never had I seen such a beautiful woman.

Moving my gaze toward the servants, I said, "Thank you." It didn't seem like much, but as I was unaccustomed to giving voice to any appreciation, it was a great deal.

8

"The celebratory dinner begins in thirty minutes," another servant declared. "It would be wise to be seated soon, before the food is served."

I silently followed the women out of the bathroom. The gown was just a tad too long, and I started to trip over the hem. But I carried myself well enough that no one would notice.

The servants led me down the hallway, and I saw many groups of guests, all dressed in fine fabrics of varying colors. Other than my feathers, I didn't feel like such an outsider anymore. I felt like I actually belonged amongst the finely dressed for once.

Continuing down the hall, the servants and I turned into the large dining hall, which made me stop in my tracks. The ceiling was high, and a dozen small tables dotted the room. At the front stood a long table decorated with place settings and fine table runners. Due to the low lighting, I felt as though I were standing in the snow as the sun sank below the horizon; it cast a dreamy look across the room.

I quickly shook my head and caught up with the servants. I dodged around a few different people, and suddenly stopped running once I realized that everyone else was walking. If I was supposed to be sophisticated, I needed to act like it.

As I approached the group of servants, I again glanced at the long table at the front of the room. A few people were already sitting down and I stopped.

A regal man was sitting at the head of the table, his dark hair perfectly coiffed. His skin, which was the color of snow, was smooth, and almost glowed in the low lighting. Even from far away, his hazel eyes glimmered as they suddenly landed on me.

The general briefly smiled at me, and I dropped my gaze to my shoes and started walking. I made my way to the group of servants, who showed me to my seat.

"Alice, this is The Mad Hatter," one of them said, gesturing to him.

The general immediately rose from his chair. He was much taller than I had imagined. He swiftly took a few steps forward and bowed before me. With shy smiles, the servants quickly left me alone.

"It is an honor to meet with you, Alice," the general said, his voice smooth and rich. "But call me The Mad Hatter, please. I hate all the formalities. I hate the term *General.* I also believe in calling it like it is. I am *mad*, after all." A wicked smile mastered his face.

I could only blink. Even though I had murdered hundreds of men who looked just like The Mad Hatter, I could hardly stand in his presence without feeling like I was a mere peasant girl.

"Please, come join me," The Mad Hatter said as he pulled out a chair next to his. "We have just fifteen minutes before the dinner begins." I walked closer, trying to steady my breathing. "My cousin speaks highly of you. I hear you are a fierce warrior, worthy of any opponent."

I nodded and tried to smile without seeming awkward. I carefully sat down in my chair, remembering to keep my head up.

"Thank you for giving me the invitation for tonight," I said quietly.

"It is an honor to have you here," The Mad Hatter said, leaning towards me with a small smile. "After all, you are the only female soldier in my army, and you led our men to victory. My cousin Rabbit also speaks of marriage. He believes you were sent to us for a reason. So a small dinner is the least I could do to honor you."

"What would be the *most* you could do to honor me?" I suddenly asked.

He looked thoughtful for a moment. "I would probably give you jewels, beautiful gowns, and anything else you desired. Although I feel you would want none."

I laughed and felt a blush creep onto my face, making it pinker than it already was. The light conversation with The Mad Hatter put my nerves at ease. I had never imagined him being so personable. We spoke of past battles for several moments until we were interrupted by Rabbit's entrance.

I turned my head and made eye contact. Rabbit gave me a warm smile and gracefully made his way to stand by my side.

I stood up to greet him. "Hello, sir. Thank you for having me." The words of my greeting came out far more formally than I intended.

He smiled again and looked at The Mad Hatter. "I see you have met my cousin."

I nodded. "Yes."

Rabbit pulled out my chair a bit more and motioned for me to sit again. "Please have a seat."

I did as he asked and he took the seat next to mine.

The Mad Hatter stood up to start the celebration. "My guests, I am honored to stand before you. We are here for celebration, for thanks and joy. We are also here to acknowledge a great soldier amongst our army." His gaze went to me as he raised his glass. "We are here to celebrate the strength of Alice." The room cheered in unison.

I smiled and nodded at all the toasts. I tried to hide how uncomfortable I felt. Rabbit must have sensed my discomfort because he reached under the table and grabbed my hand. The small squeeze he offered did wonders to calm my raging nerves.

"So tonight," The Mad Hatter continued, "we feast. Tomorrow, we conquer." More cheers broke out as the general returned to his seat.

For the next ten minutes, Rabbit and I launched into casual conversation, and I found myself laughing more now than I ever had before. Soon, the meal was brought out, and I had to restrain myself from eating like an animal with all the variety of food that was offered to me. In between bites, Rabbit and I talked, and I found myself getting more and more comfortable with him as the night went on.

Eventually, The Mad Hatter paused the meal to declare the victory of the army in more detail.

Everyone let out a cheer and I sat stiffly, setting my food aside even though I was still starving. I hesitantly stood up when The Mad Hatter called upon me to recognize me for my service to the army.

Then everyone went back to eating, and I quickly finished the rest of my meal, not caring about who saw me or how I ate.

Just as I was dabbing my mouth with a napkin, Rabbit nudged my elbow and leaned forward so that his lips were at my ear.

"Would you accompany me in getting some fresh air?" he asked quietly.

Just his lips at my ear made me shiver a little, and I nodded. Rabbit grinned, then stood up and offered me his hand. I took it with a controlled smile and we slipped out of the dining hall without anyone paying much notice.

Once we were back in the hallway, I stumbled a little. The wine I had been drinking caused my mind to spin.

"Where are we going?" I asked when Rabbit squeezed my hand and started pulling me down the hallway.

"Somewhere quiet," he said in a whisper, urging me to follow him.

I followed with no resistance, and we lightly ran down the hallway. Almost everyone in the house was enjoying dinner in the dining hall, and they were all eating and talking, so no one would really notice our absence. In the dimly lit halls, we hurried. I slipped down the polished stone in my soft slippers, let out a curse, then covered my mouth with my hand. Rabbit shushed me with a soft smile on his lips. Then he pulled me down another hallway that was lit by torches and seemed a little more elegant than the rest of the building.

"Where are we going?" I asked with a smile.

Rabbit merely shook his head, then pulled me into a room. He drew the stone door back into place and leaned against it.

"Where are we?" I asked quietly.

The room we were standing in held a lavish bed with four posts, a canopy stretched over it. The walls were decorated with ornate artwork, and the floor was covered with a plush rug. The room's lighting was provided by two torches.

"This is my room," Rabbit said, gesturing around it with a sweep of his arm. He removed his boots and sat down on the foot of his bed, inviting me to join him.

With my heart rate spiking, and feeling a little dizzy from the wine, I sat down beside him. I almost moaned in delighted pleasure when he put his arm around my shoulders. I leaned slightly into him, feeling my face grow warm. I assumed this was what they would call a 'cuddle', something I had never done in my life, and I enjoyed the simple comfort of it.

"Here, lie back with me," he said softly, leaning back on his bed. He fell back against the pillows at the head of the bed and I joined him, leaning my head against his chest.

Rabbit smelled like spice and wine, and I inhaled deeply. The wine I'd drunk caused my body to feel heavy, and my head even more so.

"Thank you for coming tonight," he murmured against the top of my head, his fingers gently running through my tresses. "I know this isn't a setting you are used to, and I know I asked a lot of you to do this."

"I wore a dress for you," I teased. "And I even bathed!"

Rabbit laughed loudly. "Well, thank goodness for that!"

"But all the servants, the big house, the extravagance... it just isn't me. I grew up with all of that and hated it," I admitted.

"May I ask you something?"

I simply nodded.

"Why did you leave the Penna?"

I froze.

He must have felt my tension. "Why does my question bother you?"

"The past is where I left it. I don't want to revisit it." I held my breath, hoping that my answer would be sufficient enough and he wouldn't press any further.

"But our past is what made us become who we are. I want to know what there is to know about you, Alice."

"You've told me nothing of your past," I countered, hoping to divert the conversation.

"What do you want to know? There's nothing I won't tell you," he offered. He didn't wait for me to ask but began on his own. "All my family is dead besides my cousin The Mad Hatter. He and I grew up together as children, and stayed together even after the raid. Penna soldiers came into my village when I was ten years old and killed everyone in sight. There was no mercy for anyone. Women were killed. Children. Everyone. The Mad Hatter was sixteen at the time, and managed to sneak us out safely as everything we knew and everyone we loved burned down to nothing but ash." He paused and held my wrist, running a fingertip along my feathers. "We vowed that day to kill all who had feathers. All." He took a deep breath. "And the day I saw you, I would have killed you like I did all the others, except something stopped me."

"What stopped you?"

Rabbit shook his head slowly. "I'm not sure. I

just couldn't bring myself to do it, or allow anyone else to." He ran his hand through his tousled hair while he stared up at the ceiling. "With a thirst for revenge, The Mad Hatter and I fought our way up the ranks of the Cyans, and eventually became the leaders. Years of war, and many deaths."

"Do you feel you got your revenge?" I asked softly.

"No. I don't think I ever will. No matter how many Penna I killed, the hole in my heart just grew bigger and bigger." He took a deep breath and turned toward me. "So what about you? Are you seeking revenge? What makes you kill the way you do?"

I shrugged. "I don't know. It's all I have ever done. I'm different from you in that the Penna do not allow emotion to come into play. Revenge is most certainly an emotion, and a deadly one at that."

Rabbit nodded. "That it is. But something must have made you fight. And you still haven't told me why you decided to leave. What happened? Did they do something to you?"

"No, they never did anything to me. I grew up seeing a side of the Penna that I hated, and..." I sighed, hating that I had opened up about my past as much as I had done. "I'm a soldier who left the Penna. Can't we just leave it at that?"

"Do you not trust me?" he asked, looking skeptical at my resistance. "Do you have something so awful to hide that you fear I will judge you?"

I took a deep breath. "Another time. I have had a wonderful evening, and I just want to spend this time with you, and not allow any storm clouds of my past to take it all away. Can we have this conversation another time? Please?"

There was a long moment of silence. I looked up at him, and before I knew it, Rabbit's lips were pressed against mine, and I felt my body catch fire. I froze for a brief moment but let my hands wander up to caress his face. My hair fell down my back as soon as he unfastened the jeweled clip that had been placed there with care.

I drank him in, inhaling his sweet scent and reveling in the taste of his lips. He tasted like wine, mint, and the food we had at dinner. I could not get enough of his essence.

"I've missed you," he whispered against my mouth. "I've been so busy since returning to Danis that I've neglected you. I'm sorry."

"You run an army. I completely understand. Besides," I said as I kissed his lips again softly, "it has allowed me to train freely without you watching my every move."

He smiled against the kiss. "Do you feel I smothered you with my overprotectiveness?"

"No, not smothered. Protected, cared for, yes. But not smothered. I hate to admit this," I paused to come up with the right words, "but I enjoy it. And I have missed it."

"Ahhh," he chuckled, "is that a hint of submission I see in my strong-willed soldier?"

I giggled, the unfamiliar sound surprising me. It suddenly dawned on me that I had never giggled, or even laughed freely. A Penna soldier did not do such things. It felt nice. It felt really nice.

"It's all right to laugh. I like seeing this side of you," he said as he swiped a wayward hair away from my eye. "You don't have to be a soldier all the time. The softness in you is beautiful."

"You find me beautiful?" I had never been told such a thing.

"Very much so. I have never seen a woman who has the power to take me down with a sword as well as with her looks."

The heat from my core rose to my face. I swallowed hard as I tried to comprehend the emotions rushing through me. What were they? What did I feel? Was this love? Was this what love felt like? Could a Penna truly feel love? Was that what the powerful feeling of warmth inside me was? Love?

Rabbit pulled me closer and whispered, "God, I've missed seeing you daily. Your presence gives me hope. You make me happy, Alice. You give me light in a very dark time."

"You do the same for me," I admitted openly.

"I have not been able to free you from my thoughts since our last meeting."

I blushed with the memory of his hand on my naked bottom. "Yes. The memory is seared in my mind."

He kissed me deeper, forcing his tongue in my mouth only to be met with my sensual response. He rolled me onto my back in one swift move, never breaking the kiss. He ran along the curve of my body with his hand, softness mixed with strength.

"I find your archery commendable, but nothing compares to your womanly shape. I've never seen or touched a woman with muscles like yours, yet they are met with such soft and gentle curves. The combination..." He growled as he kissed me harder.

As if we had done this dance a thousand times, Rabbit removed my clothing effortlessly, followed by his own. A single beat was never missed as he kissed with fervor like no other. In mere moments, we both lay nude, entwined in each other's arms.

He kissed my neck, gently nipping at my skin as his palm caressed my breast. The heat of his hand warmed my firm nipple and shot a bolt of desire to my core. My body melted against his weight. Kiss by kiss, he lowered himself down until his face was inches from my sex.

"I would like to taste you. I want the taste of you on my tongue." He didn't wait for permission, but rather kissed my pussy, followed by licking my throbbing clit.

I tensed at the invasion. Part of me wanted to stop, and the other part wanted the feeling to never end. He swirled his tongue in circles, lapping up every sign of my arousal. I moaned with complete abandon. My body seemed possessed by Satan himself. I had absolutely no power against him. Lick after lick, Rabbit brought my body to another level. Just when I believed I could take no more, he thrust his finger past the lips of my pussy. In and out he plunged, pulling gasps and moans from me.

"Rabbit! Oh, Rabbit." For the first time in my life, I had lost control, and I didn't care anymore.

He thrust his finger while sucking on me at the same time. When he pressed his finger as deep as I thought possible, an explosion of lights went off in my body. Uncontrollable waves of ecstasy rocked my trembling frame. My pussy pulsated around his finger, covering it in my completion.

Before the last wave washed over me, he flipped me around so I was lying on my stomach.

He pulled out his wet finger and rubbed it on my anus.

I tensed and bucked upward. He pressed me back down and whispered, "Allow me."

His command was followed by him pulling my juices from my pleasured sex and spreading it around my rosebud once more. Before I could comprehend the invasive nature of the act, he pressed his dripping finger past my puckered hole. I screamed out in a mixture of shock, pain, and animalistic desire.

"Relax, Alice. This is where you learn to submit to me."

I tossed my head from side to side as he pressed his finger even deeper into my ass. "I don't think I can. I—"

Pressing his finger even further, he then pulled it out halfway. He pumped it in and out in a slow, sensual motion. "Feel your body become mine. Feel how your body wants nothing more than to succumb to my touch." Thrusting his finger in a few more times, he asked, "Who do you belong to, Alice? Who?"

There was no hesitation. No question in my mind. "You! I will always belong to you!"

"Will you submit to me?"

I paused. The hesitation caused a searing slap to my ass, and then another.

"Say you will submit to me."

I remained silent as he continued to press his finger in and out of my tight channel. My silence brought on several more swats. He continued to spank me as he fucked my ass with his finger, over and over again as I moaned his name.

"You will end this night in complete surrender to me," he growled as he continued to spank and punish my bottom hole.

With every spank, I couldn't help but tense around his finger. The stretch brought on sensations that clouded my mind. I wanted Rabbit to completely take me. I wanted to feel his cock pressed deep within me more than I had ever wanted anything before. With each spank, I longed for more. My ass blazed as the spanking continued. Swats echoed off the stone walls, mixed with my gasps and whimpers.

As his palm connected with my sensitive sit-spot, I cried out, "Rabbit! It stings!"

He responded by spanking me several more times in the exact same spot. He pressed his finger deeper into my bottom hole, causing my ass to buck against his hand. Juices soaked my pussy and coated my inner thigh. An inferno of hunger consumed me. My body felt starved for his touch even though my mind questioned the taboo of such an act.

"Please! I beg you!" What I was begging for, I wasn't quite sure.

Pure submission lurked beneath the shadows of my soul. I wanted to allow it, and yet I fought it desperately from emerging.

He spanked me harder than he had ever done before. "Submit!" The final command was all it took.

I grabbed the sheets of his bed in my fists and screamed between my teeth, "Yes! Yes, I will submit to you."

He removed his finger and flipped me onto my back. I felt the mattress compress as he kneeled before my face and placed his hard cock to my lips. I looked up and into his eyes. No words needed to be said. I opened up my mouth and allowed his cock to lie against my tongue. My natural instinct was to pleasure him. Nothing got in the way of how badly I wanted to make him scream out my name. Watching bliss blanket his face filled me with a purpose I had not known existed. As I sucked up and down his ready dick, I fully submitted to Rabbit. Up and down I moved my mouth, until I was rewarded by my name escaping his lips in the most passionate of ways. My name never sounded as good as it did the moment it slipped from his lips.

I added my hand and began to pump his cock

while licking all around it. His body shook and tensed, and with a large groan, Rabbit spent his satisfaction into the back of my throat. I swallowed his seed with the gratification of the most submissive of women.

WHAT SEEMED LIKE HOURS LATER, I stirred and my eyes fluttered open. Plush velvet was wrapped around my body, and I saw Rabbit asleep on the bed beside me. Bolting up, I glanced around the room, briefly forgetting where I was.

Rabbit stirred, but didn't wake. He merely rolled onto his side, his dark hair falling in his face.

I carefully stood up from the bed, careful to not wake him, and glanced in one of the mirrors hanging on the wall. I ran my fingers through my hair to brush out all the knots.

"Alice?"

I whipped around to see Rabbit sitting up in bed, rubbing his forehead with his hand. He blinked sleepily and looked at me with a small smile playing at his lips.

"What time is it?" I asked as I turned away from the mirror to sit down on the edge of the bed. "What will people say if they find me in your room?"

"It doesn't matter. What we do is our own concern." He smiled. "Warriors bed often, and since you are a warrior, you should not worry about your reputation," he teased.

"Yes, but I am soon to be a bride to Commander Rabbit. Wouldn't reputation matter then?" I countered, matching his playful smile.

"Your virtue is still intact."

I blushed at the memory of how close we had gotten. "Yes, but how would anyone know that?"

He stood up, stretching slowly. "Very well, let's join the party again." Rabbit slipped on his clothes and then helped me dress. He ran his hand through his hair once more and looked at me with soft eyes.

I nodded and followed him out of his room, keeping close behind him. Without saying anything, he took my hand and gripped it tightly. I did not say anything else.

When we turned into the main hallway, I expected there to be guests gathering about. But when Rabbit and I peeked through the door, I saw the entire crowd still in the dining hall.

"I guess it is not too late," Rabbit whispered to me. "We must have only been alone for a few hours." He squeezed my hand reassuringly. "The Mad Hatter enjoys long parties that go late into the night."

I nodded and pulled my brown hair to one side, running my fingers through it. He turned back to me with a warm smile.

"I would like to see you again soon, Alice. Besides just in battle," Rabbit told me, taking both of my hands.

I stared at him. "I'm a soldier. We train on a daily basis, and I live in the quartering area which is far from your home. And you're busy rebuilding your army. It's going to be hard to see each other. That is, until we do go to battle."

Rabbit stared at me for a long moment, until I started to get uncomfortable.

"What's wrong?" I asked quietly.

"I would like you to live in the house with me." Before I could argue, he said, "You would live in your own room if you want. That way, we won't be far from each other. I feel it is safer for you to be here, anyway. You are the only woman among many... lonely... men."

"But how would I train?" I demanded. "I'm sure that your cousin, of all people, would want to keep me in his army. After all, I was just given honors for helping to lead his army to victory."

Rabbit nodded. "You could train in the courtyard, as will I. You would still be a loyal part of this army."

I paused long enough to consider the proposal.

"I'm not sure your cousin would agree to it. He might reject this idea. It will look like you are playing favorites."

"I am. You are my favorite." He smiled a toothy grin, which made me smile in return.

"Rabbit." I shoved his shoulder playfully. "I'm serious."

"He will see it my way, I'm sure. You are our prized soldier, after all," he said with a devilish wink that made butterflies erupt in my stomach.

I nodded a little and glanced down at my shoes. "Will you allow me to think this over? I fear the other men would not like the special treatment. I don't want to seem like I'm weaker."

"It is for your safety."

I nodded. "Yes." I looked deep into his eyes, and raised my eyebrows in question. "And for no other reason?"

Rabbit used his finger to lift up my chin. He pressed a short kiss to my lips, pulling away with both of us smiling. "For your safety, my dark feather. Allow me to protect the army's prized possession. *My* prized possession." He kissed me again before adding, "But that's not really the whole truth."

"Ahh, so the truth finally comes out," I teased.

"You are safe at camp. I made sure of it by asking Cheshire to keep an eye out for you. No man will dare come near you knowing that Cheshire is ready to attack on my command."

I wasn't sure if I should speak of the conversation Cheshire and I had exchanged only a few hours earlier. Though I didn't really feel the need to withhold the fact that we'd spoken, I wasn't sure if Cheshire would consider it a breach of confidence. I also didn't know if he'd consider that his confession that he wished to have feathers might be seen as a sign of weakness. No, I would do nothing to possibly cause even a modicum of his commander's respect to be taken from a fellow soldier. My decision made, I said, "Cheshire? Why Cheshire? I need protection from *him*. He hates me."

Rabbit chuckled. "He hates everyone." He laughed again. "But I wouldn't want anyone else—except you—to stand by my side. He has saved my life many times, and I will forever call him my friend."

I huffed. "Well, good thing I didn't kill him," I said with a smile. "It would have been unfortunate to kill your friend."

"He'll be your friend someday. Just give him time. Already the men are impressed with you, and with time, they will all see you for the wonderful, and powerful woman you are." He spun me around and playfully swatted me on the butt. "But yes, I will give you some time. Not much, but some."

"And if I say no?" I asked as I placed my hands on my hips and played the part of a mischievous brat. Every emotion flowing through me was foreign, but I loved it. It was refreshing to be so carefree in a place that was anything but. Rabbit allowed me to step away from darkness and see a light, if even for a short time.

He gave me an impish smile. "Then I will just have to convince you to change your mind. I am your commander, after all. I may just give you a direct order. And like any good soldier, you would follow your commands. Am I right?"

My heart soared with our playful banter and my face nearly hurt from how big I was smiling. "Yes, sir. I will always follow your command."

9

Slipping out of the first dress I had worn in a long time, I ran my hand down the fabric. Yes, the color had reminded me of blood, and yet now, the richness of the deep, vibrant crimson would always bring to mind elegance and... well, femininity. Removing the ruby necklace and setting it next to the dress, I shook my head. Neither of those things had a purpose in my life. Pulling on the clothing I had worn only a few hours earlier, I reminded myself that jewels, no matter how priceless, and a dress, no matter how beautiful, would not keep me safe. My training, my skills as a warrior, my ability to nock an arrow into my bow, sending it true to its target—as easily as the servants had wielded their pots to paint my face—those traits would keep me alive.

Rabbit insisted on walking me back to camp after we'd left the dinner and I had changed. After the spanking, and the intimate influence of submission, and with his hand even now pressed hotly against my flesh, I no longer had the same desire to protest his dictate. His kind words and soft touch afterwards had earned it. My feelings for Rabbit remained confusing, but one thing I was sure of was my intense respect for him.

"Do you know where the Penna are keeping our men?" I asked as we strolled under the moonlight. The battle a few days back had resulted in three of the Cyan men being captured.

"We don't."

"They know how to torture answers out of the bravest of men. I fear our location is no longer safe."

He nodded. "We have never been safe. If the Penna want to march toward us, I say let them. We will be ready."

"We should be on the attack, not the defense. We need to find them before they even get within several miles of here."

He leaned in closer to my face, and I moved closer as well. I watched his eyes glinting in the moonlight, hoping for another kiss like before.

"RABBIT!"

A voice shouted from a few hundred yards

away. I thought I recognized it to be Cheshire calling.

"RABBIT!"

Rabbit and I hurried toward the shouting and saw a beaten body lying naked in the bitter night snow. I recognized the man's face.

"Garrett," I said softly under my breath. Poor Garrett. He was always one of the nicer soldiers. I breathed a solemn sigh.

Cheshire studied Rabbit and me when he saw us approach him side by side. Cheshire pointed at the dead body. "The Penna and their cowardly men killed him. They killed a man held captive."

"Did he say anything before you saw him like this?" Rabbit asked.

"Not a word. He stumbled here and collapsed," Cheshire replied. "Maybe if you hadn't been too busy deciding where to 'stick your dagger', none of this would have happened."

"How dare you speak to me like that!" Rabbit tried to lift his sword free but I stopped him fast, resting my hand on his wrist. Garrett and Cheshire had been close. His anger was understandable.

"Sir! The Penna are approaching!" one of the soldiers called out from the distance.

In a blur, we all grabbed our weapons and headed to the wall to face our enemy.

Rabbit asked me to stay while he and a small group of others met with the Penna.

"No."

He frowned, but I knew that was the end of it. I was going.

I could sense that one of Rabbit's top priorities was to protect me, and when he didn't feel like he was doing so well, it upset him. But now, I was just as much a part of this as he was.

"I wish you would not come," Rabbit snapped in one last desperate—yet futile—attempt at keeping me back.

"I know," I replied. I also knew he didn't actually expect me to remain back.

Side by side, we all carried bright torches, though the deepest part of the night had already passed and a new day would dawn soon. Our broad swords gleamed as they hung slung across our backs. Our snowmobiles gathered speed through the shifting valley of snow.

Rabbit held his hand up and commanded all of his riders to stop. A shimmer of something loomed up ahead.

The Penna came on snowmobiles from the depths of the icy land. They were wary. The heavy armor they were coated in suggested it. In the distance, some of the enemy sat on their machines in front of many others, who hung back even further. The Cyan army never dishonored the diplomacy intended to discuss terms, but the Penna seemed nervous. Over the past month, many rumors had gone through the campgrounds about the Penna's unfaltering nerve. People believed they were unstoppable, unwavering. That wasn't what I saw tonight.

"They want to talk," Rabbit said to me.

"Do you think there are more we cannot see?" I asked. My snowmobile vibrated loudly beneath me as I spoke.

"No Penna would be foolish enough to venture out into the icy land without a powerful army. Well, except for the one sitting next to us," Cheshire muttered, coughing over his shoulder.

"Keep your words to yourself," Rabbit barked.

"Let me go with you. Let me go and talk to them," I said, driving into Rabbit's path. Rabbit looked up and faced me.

"You mean to talk sense into them? You really are mad…" Cheshire said, sliding his hands down his cheeks.

Rabbit turned his snowmobile so he could face his men. "Stay here and do not move until I give you a sign," he demanded.

The men held back, watching.

The Penna drove until they were a hundred yards from their battalions, and paused. Rabbit,

Cheshire, and I drove toward them. I recognized them instantly. One soldier was a man of considerable strength and poise. He was nearly twice the size of any man in our army, and had a loose, shoddy-looking cloth eye patch over one eye. No one knew why, and no one asked him about it. He didn't speak much unless drunk. He carried a massive double-sided battle-axe no one else could even hoist. The other soldier by his side was almost the complete opposite—small, agile, loquacious, cunning. He had always preferred knives. Both men were deadly.

Cheshire was a master of tongues and diplomacy—even if not with me. If there was any chance we would see the Penna leave without bloodshed, he would be the man to secure it.

"What do these men want? There are not enough of them for battle. They are outnumbered," Rabbit said.

Their snowmobiles moved together in perfect formation, as if the very machines were demanding we understand the gravity of this unexpected assembly.

"I have not dealt with them personally. But this is out of the ordinary. Is it not, Alice?" Cheshire asked.

"It is unlike the Penna to come only to discuss," I agreed.

"Then why are we here? More importantly, why are they here?" Rabbit asked.

The closer we moved to the solitary Penna, the stronger the pungent smell of death became. It was almost as if the Penna had splashed their bodies with the cloying scent of decay as if to convey that while they were willing to 'talk', we need not forget they were better known for slaughter. The Penna were sending a message. An orange and violet hue spread as the first rays of sunlight bled over the desolate plain. A few feet before them sat a man on a machine with a crooked smile.

As we approached the Penna, they dismounted and stood there. This was not a typical arrangement. It was customary to always stay on their snowmobiles to discuss terms.

"Dismount," their general ordered us. "We will talk."

This didn't sit well with me. I looked at Rabbit for a moment, and could see he knew how I felt. He read me well and yet, when he dismounted, Cheshire and I followed suit.

"We thought you dead, Alice." The general took in my new appearance. "So the rumors are true. You are a traitor to us just as you were a traitor to your father."

"Do you have our men?" Rabbit interrupted.

The general seemed surprised Rabbit was so bold as to interrupt him.

The general nodded. "We do. We will gladly return them in exchange for Alice. She is a traitor, and must be tried as such. Her fate is to be prosecuted, and hopefully, executed."

"She goes nowhere with you," Rabbit responded.

"You know what we want. This woman does not belong with you. Keep her, and we'll kill you *slowly*. But if you give Alice to us, we'll kill her and then the rest of your men, but *quickly*. We are merciful men, after all." The Penna all chuckled at their general's words. "Take your pick." None of the Penna seemed worried about a reaction from Rabbit, Cheshire, or me.

"Talk is over. Walk away now, or taste the sharp end of my sword," Rabbit announced.

"Very well," the general said. He came toward us with six other men in tow. It looked like a formation.

Cheshire approached slightly ahead of Rabbit and me. The general reached his hand out to grab Cheshire in what appeared to be a friendly gesture.

I had known something was off from the moment the call that the Penna were here was given, and yet had kept as silent as possible as I did not command the Cyan army. I could feel my gut coiling, my instincts protesting as I watched Cheshire reaching for the general's hand. In that split second between their flesh meeting, seeing the other Penna's hands clenching around the hilts of their swords, I screamed, "No!" My warning came too late.

The general's hand clasped around Cheshire's and pulled him in close to ensnare him while he used his other hand to unleash his short, close-combat knife. He pierced through Cheshire's midsection and was out of the way just in time to dodge a fellow Penna soldier's battle-axe coming down toward Cheshire's head, barely missing it.

"No!" I screamed again as total chaos ensued.

The other six Penna filed forward, forming a half oval around the general and raising their shields. They outnumbered us and yet we gave no quarter. Rabbit peeled six throwing knives out from where they were strapped around his tunic, and deftly put four of them in the legs of one of the men. I charged forward and swung my sword with a centrifugal force so massive that it cleaved one man in half. His body falling caused another man to stumble and yet he managed to stay on his feet. Rabbit sprang onto the man with knives in his legs, pushing a knife into his heart and twisting.

The general and his remaining four Penna mounted their snowmobiles and fled. Rabbit sent two more knives whispering through the air, both landing in the back of one of the men. The man tumbled into the snow while his snowmobile surged into the icy vastness. Rabbit pulled out the knives he'd planted in the bodies, and after wiping them off on his pants, he placed them back in the straps lining his tunic. I ran to Cheshire as he gasped for breath, my sword still drawn. Rabbit came to stand next to me, taking large breaths.

"Come on, Cheshire. Don't die," I gently ordered the man who now lay in my lap. Cheshire had been so cruel to me, and yet had shared his desire for feathers, and in his dying breaths, I could see a softness so long hidden under his rough façade.

Cheshire's stomach looked awful. Blood spurted with every beat of his heart. I saw his eyes drifting.

Rabbit bent down and smacked his face. "Listen to the woman. Fight!"

I tried to comfort him as he went.

"Cheshire. Cheshire!" Rabbit cried.

I rubbed Cheshire's hand, and he smirked at Rabbit. "I've never been good at following your orders," he said between coughs.

"Well it's about time you fucking learn!" Rabbit almost pleaded rather than commanded. "Fight death just like you would fight any of those God damn Penna."

I pressed my hand on the bleeding wound, doing my best to hinder the bleeding, but I knew he was losing too much blood. I had seen enough men die in battle to know that Cheshire would soon die. And judging by the pain that washed over Rabbit's face, he too knew that death would be the end result.

Cheshire reached down and pulled my bloody hand from his wound, allowing the blood to flow freely. He looked into my eyes and said, "I was wrong about you, Alice. You have proven to every one of us that you are a soldier worth respecting. I am honored to have fought beside you." He coughed, blood seeping out of the corners of his mouth. "I shouldn't have been so hard," he coughed again, "none of us should have been so hard." He held my hand with whatever energy he surely had left in his body and squeezed. "But we all believe you are our dark feather sent here to lead the Cyan to victory. And Rabbit..." He paused while he swallowed back the pool of blood forming in the back of his throat. "Fight beside Rabbit. Protect him, help him, but mostly... love him." When his fingers loosed his hold on my hand, I yanked a feather from my wrist and pressed it into his palm, closing his bloody fingers around it.

"I will, I give you my word."

"I already feel warmer..." He smiled one last time, and the light faded from his eyes.

It wasn't until then that I noticed I was surrounded by soldiers. Grief conquered each one. Unlike the Penna, these men were not ashamed to show their pain. They weren't ashamed to cry and mourn someone they cared so deeply about. We had lost Cheshire. We had all lost a respected soldier, and a friend.

"They wanted death," Rabbit said, his voice cracking with pain.

"They got it," I replied. "They wanted to send a message that they know where we are."

Defeated, Rabbit picked up Cheshire's lifeless body and carried him back to our encampment, followed by every man who had once fought beside Cheshire. Rabbit placed him gently in the snow, sorrow blanketing his face and tears in his eyes.

"He could be a real son of a bitch, but a worthy and loyal fighter," he declared. "He was my friend, and he did not deserve to die under such deceit. Those fucking cowards will pay!"

I knew the worst still lay ahead, and all of Rabbit's men were ready to lay siege.

"I'm so sorry. They wanted me," I said as a deep sorrow washed over me.

Rabbit touched my cheek, wiping a stray tear from my eye. "Whatever happens, happens to all of us."

"They just want me. Maybe it's best for you to surrender me. If you push hard and negotiate, then maybe they would give you your men back in return."

Rabbit shook his head. "My men are dead. Or at least, they will be. There is no bargaining with the Penna. They killed Cheshire in what was supposed to be a peaceful parley." He wiped at another tear escaping my eyes. "We fight. We stay strong. We stay together."

No matter how hard he tried to convince me, I knew many of them would not survive this fight. "Cheshire died because of me," I said.

"Cheshire died because of the Penna. Not you."

I saw such pain in his eyes as he reached for the shovel one of his men brought over. He allowed no one to offer assistance in digging the hole to lay Cheshire to rest in. He attacked the frozen ground as if it were the general of the Penna, and didn't pause until Cheshire was lowered into the ground.

When it was all done, I just put my arm around him and said, "Vengeance."

Rabbit turned to face his grieving men. "All that matters now is we find out how to ambush their encampment." He turned to me and nodded.

"Yes, vengeance in the name of Cheshire, Garrett, and all the men we lost," Rabbit shouted to us all.

Cheers rang back in return as the storm clouds came rolling over, dark and bloated in the breaking dawn.

"It is decided. We prepare, and at week's end, we head for revenge."

10

The thundering sounds of a vengeful Cyan army swept violently through the icy land. The collapse of silence surrounded the Penna below. From the midday sun over a frozen landscape came the war cries of many. Some were from the Penna in warning, and others came from the Cyan, who hollered as they prepared for battle. The Penna armed themselves with weapons and courage to fight what was—hopefully for the Cyan—to be the Penna's last battle for some time. All the Cyan had to do was kill the Penna general, and the effect would be crippling. They were outnumbered and consumed from all angles. Still, as they watched the army of Cyan coming to attack, the fight was inevitable. From the middle of the Penna camp came the ringing of the horns. The soldiers came together, as did all able-bodied men. The blood-thirsty Cyans were coming!

Rabbit didn't want to sneak in on them. He wanted them to see death approaching. He wanted them to see their demise advancing with every single inch the Cyans took as they attacked. The Cyan were out for blood, and Rabbit wanted to make damn sure the Penna saw the hunger.

"Some of you will die," Rabbit called out to his men when we stopped on top of the highest ridge. "Some will be captured and most likely tortured. But for the memory of Cheshire and all our fallen men, you will die with honor. Soldiers, now is your time—the time for vengeance is today!" The snowmobile Rabbit was riding took off. From that very moment, the battle had commenced.

From the freezing land, hundreds of Cyan soldiers rushed to the bottom of the ridge, some with snowmobiles, others without. However, all were armed, and all were ravenous.

Balls of flame shot through the roofs of the Penna's tents. The fabric caught instantaneously, and quickly spread to nearby structures. The Cyan forces on snowmobiles arrived soon after, throwing spears and piercing the frontlines. Undecipherable chants roared after each target was brought down. We maneuvered so smoothly, it was impossible to catch sight of our front halves. The tents and structures collapsed one by one, folding in towards the center. The berserk aura of the Cyan seeking vengeance for our fallen comrades brushed through the Penna's camp and conquered it completely. More areas of the camp were set on fire. Flames rose high in the sky. The oxygen supply had been almost consumed, adding the threat of carbon dioxide poisoning. However, as crazed attackers, we acted as though we needed no air to live; only the search for justice filled our bodies to satisfaction. We continued on.

War cries became screams of death. Blood flowed from their bodies, painting the white red. If ever there would be the scent of death in Wonderland, it would only come in two forms—first, when Death himself stands behind you, waiting to strike. The other time is much like this time, when no form of true Penna life existed. Wonderland would soon be a barren and icy wasteland.

The clouds covered the sun and signs of life withered in the flames, along with everything. There was almost nothing left of this once fortified stronghold.

"Forward!" someone shouted. "Forward!"

The rush of battle cries, the sprint to their deaths—it was almost too much. I could see rocks and arrows all around my feet. The Cyan soldiers, friends I had grown to care for, were fighting for their lives, fighting for what they believed in. There were men, fathers, and sons shouting and dying in front of me.

Rabbit ran up behind me and held the shield above both our heads. Rocks and arrows were denting and sticking into it. His arm weakened against the assault. He winced when something hit the shield. "Behind you!" Rabbit warned.

I spun quickly and my knife slid through a charging man's throat, his eyes staring at mine in terror as he fell. Another Penna charged and knocked the weapon from my hand. We rolled around in the snow until Rabbit lifted the man while I scrambled away. The man was on top of Rabbit with a knife aimed at his face. I found a small rock and threw, barely missing him. My hands touched a familiar blade. My knife... I feared I wouldn't reach him in time. One chance. My blade sang across the space between us and found a home in the man's shoulder. He was still going. I threw another rock, hitting him in the head. His face contorted in pain, and his strength faltered for a moment. Rabbit flipped him and turned, my knife seeming to call for me to come and finish the job. I ran over, taking the knife from his shoulder. His face was red and he held his breath, fighting against Rabbit's strength while my blade slid delicately, yet ever so deadly across his throat.

More men came. I drew my sword and fought with renewed strength. I would die on my feet. A sea of bodies fighting to the death separated me from Rabbit. I couldn't breathe well. The clang of swords was deafening. I knew my vision was blurred. The man standing to my right—his head hit the ground with a thump and rolled away—and I couldn't tell if he was friend or enemy. My vision blurred even more.

Rabbit was out there somewhere. It had started with us watching each other's backs, but now I couldn't find him.

Near me, a rock encased in flames crashed and rolled through ten different people, knocking them rapidly to the ground. A sword whirred past my face, just missing my shoulder. I swung for the man who wielded it, slicing through his belly, and he fell.

Searching frantically for Rabbit, I nearly tripped over a body. His arms were sheared off, and the blood coming from where they used to be was still trickling in the snow. Death all around, I only hoped Rabbit was not one of them.

The onslaught of snowmobiles had me careening. I could barely hold my sword anymore. I could see the elite Penna wash away like a wave in front of me. The Penna were fleeing, or at least the ones who remained alive. The battle was almost won.

I turned my head to see Rabbit, a sight that nearly brought tears to my eyes. He was alive and hopping off his snowmobile after knocking the sword from his opponent's hands. Now came the point in which the general found himself facing Rabbit.

"You may have defeated my men and torn down our camp, but you will never win. The Penna will prevail and your efforts will fade into obscurity. You Cyan will be nothing." The words came powerfully from the general, but with definite trembling in the undertone.

The cold and chilling face of Rabbit was less than an inch from the face of the general. A grin appeared, only making Rabbit more terrifying in appearance. He looked up into the skies, then back down at the general as he stroked his sword along the general's throat gently.

"Where are the mighty Penna now?" Rabbit asked, with venom oozing around each word. "You killed a man under the guise of a peaceful parley. You attacked the unarmed. A battle was not engaged. Is this how the Penna act? Is this the action of *intelligent* men? Acts of a superior mankind? If your answer is yes, then I thank God I am not *intelligent* or *superior*."

"Kill me already," the general barked.

"Killing you would spare you from having to face the Penna as a loser. You are a weak man, and all will know it when you have to crawl back and lick your filthy wounds. You are no leader. You will lead your men to their deaths."

I stood nearby. Despite the words I'd heard, I was expecting to see Rabbit pull out his sword and kill the man who had ordered so many Cyan deaths. But he surprised me by getting on his snowmobile, staring down at the man he gave mercy to, as he allowed the general to run off.

The swords stopped. The thunder in the ground had left. The most elite warriors crumpled in an instant. They retreated in shame. The last drop of blood had been shed for that day.

"Alice."

Rabbit. I didn't have the strength to even say his name at the moment. My heart, my body, and my mind were all spinning, and I needed another moment to gather myself.

"Alice. Are you all right?"

I knew his arms when they wrapped around me. To feel his touch almost made me crumple at the knees. I needed him. Never before had I needed a man so much.

"I'm fine."

"Are you hurt?"

I nodded. "Yes. The wound in my leg has reopened." He quickly scanned my bloody leg with immense worry in his eyes. "But I am alive and well." I tried to reassure him. I looked into his eyes and asked in confusion, not truly understanding his actions, "Why did you let him go? You could have killed him and ended this war right then and there."

Rabbit sighed deeply. "I could have killed him, yes. And he ran like a coward knowing that fact. But even if I would have killed him, his second, or third, or even fourth in command would have taken over. The war is not over by simply killing one man."

"Then you should have let me kill him. He doesn't deserve to live!"

"Do any of us deserve to live? We are all guilty of doing the same thing as that man. He is no worse than all of us."

"But why let him live? He killed Cheshire right in front of us. He broke an unspoken rule in the conduct of war. We were in talks, not battle. He deceived us and we lost a friend because of it."

Nodding, he said, "He did. But I felt killing him would have been giving him mercy. Now he has to live with the knowledge that the Cyan are stronger.

I am stronger." He wiped my sweaty hair from my forehead and added, "The day will come when I will indeed kill him. But right now, I didn't want to kill his body. I just wanted to decimate his soul."

Rabbit swept me up into his arms and helped me to his snowmobile. He straddled the seat behind me and placed a soft kiss on my neck.

I sighed and nodded, understanding his decision. "I think Cheshire would have been very proud of you. You made him proud today."

"Not yet. But someday I will make him proud. Someday I will avenge his death in a way that does not involve killing. But until that day—"

"That day will come," I interrupted. "I never believed so before. But since meeting you, I know there isn't anything you can't do. I have faith that you will make that happen. As crazy as it might sound," I looked around at the battlefield we'd just fought on, "I feel safe. You make me feel very, very safe. You give me hope."

"I hope I always can make you feel that way." He patted my leg and started the snowmobile. "Well, for now, the battle is won. We came and achieved what we set out to do."

We leaned into each other's bodies to begin our journey home. Visions of the battle haunted me, as they always did when the adrenaline began to leave me. My body shook, my stomach churned, and I broke out in a sweat. Every awful emotion washed over me. Emotions that I didn't allow to enter while in the midst of war came flooding in. I was used to this, but it didn't make it any easier. After each fight, I paid the price. I often wondered if I was the only soldier who suffered from the aftermath soon after the dust settled, but today, as I with Rabbit and felt his body shake, and sweat bead on his clammy skin, I knew he too fought the demons of all who were killed. It was inevitable that our shields would eventually have to be lowered, and when that happened, we had to face death head on.

I thought for a moment about not making it, not being with Rabbit, and the possibility of loss. But I just closed my eyes, allowed my body to relax against a true hero, and drifted away to slumber with the clang of swords still in my ears.

11

In the middle of the night, I snuck into Rabbit's quarters. The moonlight reflected off the smooth metal of his sword which lay next to him while he snored softly into pelts of fur. Gently, I ran my fingers through his dark, coarse hair. Rabbit flipped on his side and jabbed a dagger from under his pillow against my soft neck. I didn't even muster a fretful look in my eyes.

"If I had come here to kill you, you'd be dead by now," I said with a smile.

"You and I both know it would not be that easy."

"Easy enough," I said, watching him re-sheath his sharp knife.

"What are you doing in here, Alice?" he asked

with a slight twinkle in his eye. “Is something wrong with your own tent?”

I wondered what the answer to that question was, as well. Part of it was because I couldn’t sleep, and another part of it was something I found hard to put into words.

“I miss your touch,” I confessed.

Rabbit sat up completely and wrapped his arms around me, pulling me close to him on his bed. He kissed the top of my head, my cheek, and then he softly kissed my lips.

“I miss the sting of your hand,” I continued with the confession.

He pulled away enough so he could study my face. He raised an eyebrow in response.

I made eye contact with him. I refused to let my pride get in the way of my need. “I miss the feel of submission.” I stood up without saying another word and stripped off my clothing, never breaking eye contact with Rabbit’s stare. I stood naked before him and whispered, “Spank me.”

Never in my wildest dreams would I imagine myself being so bold, so open. But I had always been one to take my destiny into my own hands. If I wanted it, I did what I had to in order to make it happen. This was no different. I wanted to surrender to Rabbit’s discipline. Giving up control made me feel more *in* control than ever before.

Rabbit adjusted his body so he was on the edge of his bed. He patted his lap, silently ordering me to obey.

Without hesitation, I laid myself across his lap and awaited his punishing touch. A loud slap bounced off the canvas of the tent, followed by another, and another. Rabbit took no time to pause between spanks. My body tensed with each searing swat, and my hands reached for the fur pelt to squeeze.

Rabbit swatted one cheek and then moved to the next. The rhythm burned my hide but soothed my soul. My mind relaxed even though my body hummed with life. The pain of the spanking made me cry out his name, but never once did I beg him to stop. I wanted more. I wanted to feel my body melt against his until we were one.

"My dark feather," he purred as he spanked. "You have shown more strength tonight than you've shown in any battle."

I squeezed my eyes shut and clenched my teeth together. The punishment almost became too much to bear. But I wanted to reach the edge and then dive headfirst. Complete submission to the man... I loved.

The resonances of a sound punishment, blended with the sounds of a sensitive, delicate, woman crying, seemed foreign to me. Never would

I show my weakness. Never would I show my pain. But in this moment, across Rabbit's lap, I allowed myself to be the softest, and the most feminine woman I could be.

When tears mixed with the sweat from my brow, Rabbit finally stopped the bare bottom spanking. He pulled me into his arms and showered me with kisses. Such softness, such tenderness from a man who could kill with ruthless abandon. Protective masculinity blended with willing femininity in that war-worn tent—a yielding love created.

I nestled into the crook of his neck. "I love you," I whispered against his skin.

Rabbit pulled back enough so he could look into my eyes. "And I love you, my perfect warrior. I have never felt such a surge in my heart before. Never before has my heart beat so hard."

He brought his lips to mine and mastered my mouth as only someone with Rabbit's power could do—fierce, powerful, but tender. Our tongues danced together, tasting the newly declared love just spoken.

"Please make love to me," I begged between the kiss.

He froze and took a deep breath. "In time."

A sharp pang attacked my heart. "No, the time

is now." I rested my hand on the bulge of his pants, feeling it flex beneath my touch.

Rabbit took another deep breath and closed his eyes. He let out a soft moan but lifted my hand and held it in his large palm. "In time," he repeated, but with less conviction.

"I belong to you, Rabbit. Claim me."

"We are not married. The idea may be archaic to the Penna, but to me, it is very important. I want to give you marriage and all that comes with that union." He helped me off his lap and reached for my clothing to dress me.

The tears stung the back of my eyes. "You reject me?"

Rabbit finished dressing me and then wrapped his arms tightly around my slumped shoulders. "I honor you. I value you. I respect you so very much."

I looked into his eyes and began to cry. "Do you not see me as a woman? Do you only see the archer before you?"

He pulled us both down to his bed. "I have never seen someone of such beauty. Yes, I very much see a woman." He brushed the loose strands of my hair behind my ears. "But I can only claim what I make mine. My bride will remain virtuous until we are united. Ancient in thinking, I'm sure.

But there was a time before the Wonderland froze when people valued love, commitment, and even sex. I wish for that time to return, and the least I can do is make that happen with you. I want a bond of the past to help us survive this dark and miserable future of bleak whiteness."

I nodded, understanding his belief. Disappointment soon was replaced with admiration.

"I feel I owe you an explanation," I said.

Rabbit kissed my head and continued to rub my back in tiny circles. "For what?"

"During the attack that killed Cheshire, the Penna said I was a traitor to the Penna as I was a traitor to my father."

He nodded. "Yes, I remember that."

I stared at him, surprised. "And you asked nothing about it?"

He smiled softly.

I took a deep, calming breath. "He spoke the truth." Tears stung the back of my eyes again, but I refused to let them fall.

Rabbit reached out and stroked the side of my face, tracing the signs of a scar. "I see it gives you pain."

I nodded and looked down at the ground. "Yes."

"Would telling me what happened ease that pain?"

"No. But I feel I owe you the truth regardless."

I paused a moment and could see worry in Rabbit's eyes. The unknown had to be attacking his curiosity and fear. I took another deep breath and began the long, painful, but true story.

EVERYONE HAD FLOCKED to the great hall, for after recent battles, my father—the Penna general—was due an outstanding celebration. The faded notes of a string quartet could be heard faintly through my bedroom door. I saw a stark full moon and knew something was looming. To be honest, I was quite pleased the worst of it had come to an end. Months before, my father's men, carrying out his orders, had thundered through the waving valleys of Old Montana. In their wake, they left nothing but high burning fires and bodies of dust on the southwestern terrain of a frozen state that no longer existed.

My servant no longer waited in the wings and began to speak as I brushed through my hair. "Come on, Alice," she said. "Whatever is bothering you, you need to shake off. We just had a huge victory."

But when all is said and done, was it a victory? I thought. Women and children slaughtered as the fire fed upon their flesh. I had never witnessed it, of course. My father kept me training, saying I wasn't ready. I was never ready in his eyes.

After closing my eyes briefly, I painted a fake smile on my face and left my room to join the party.

I took a pause when the strong scent of booze and sex wafted in my face. All those at the party were in the midst of imbibing rivers of red wine, dancing, and some were engaging in sex. Public displays of nudity were common at my father's parties. Dark and eerie violin music played throughout the hollow corridor, adding a thick level of lust to the atmosphere. The erotic song of the violin almost seemed hypnotic. An empty seat, right next to my father, had been left for me. Beside my father's chair sat Blaxton, his next in command. Not slowed by frost or ice, Blaxton was wholly terrifying.

My father was a man of heft, with sunburned pink skin and a thick gray beard like that of aged sheep's wool. It was only the two of us. My mother's death, when it happened, was sudden.

I remembered walking in and feeling her cold, dead fingers. When my father found me weeping at her side, he told me tears were not befitting of a Penna and I was never to cry again over someone's death. He showed no sadness, no emotion, and absolutely no love. When my mother died, I noticed Blaxton's face was cast with utter disgust. Blaxton eyed my father with rough glances. He didn't even bother to conceal it. I knew my father had played a part in her death. Everything in my soul knew he was only surviving in a place of darkness and cold. My innocent mother was just another victim in his cruel rampage of power.

I sat down next to my father and watched the grinding of bodies, the heavy drinking, and the laughter of the drunk—having started at dusk. As the hour grew late, their merry antics only grew sillier, almost as if they came down with a rising fever. Polished trays of silver lined a table from end to end. Smoked and spiced swine rested in the center of the table. Pastries made with blue-green algae were everywhere to display our great wealth.

My father grabbed a fistful of dried blue-green algae used to season our food and crushed it between his fingers. He spoke, "Eat up, men! We need to keep our strength up. There are more Cyan to kill!"

Overjoyed, a slump-shouldered soldier hollered with a swig of wine in his hand. "Under your leadership, we will kill every last one of them."

The grizzled looking Blaxton placed a gleaming knife on the side of his plate and raised his voice above the noise. "We celebrate a victory over innocent men, and for that we are proud? The last attack was on innocent villagers. They did not deserve to die."

My father slammed down his fist and glared at Blaxton with a flushed red face and wild eyes. He lurched slightly forward over the table. "You would be advised to keep your opinions to yourself." I watched him bite a chunk out of the roasted meat.

"What I mean—and so do many of my men—is that hacking down unarmed villagers who are already as good as dead from cold and starvation, is simply an easy target."

I knew Blaxton was no doubt loyal to the Penna, but I'd never seen him act so bold.

My father's jaw stiffened. "Their lives and their land became forfeit when they decided not to join the Penna. You are either with us, or against us."

Blaxton simply raised his glass with a haughty expression on his face. "If you say so, General."

My father seemed shocked, as if he could hardly believe what he'd heard. He looked to the other soldiers in attendance. "*If I say so*? If I say so, we will drink their boiled blood and dance on their bones. All non-Penna people will know their place."

I grabbed my father's forearm—clenching it equally soft and hard— before trying to think of something to say. "Let's enjoy the party. We won the last battle, and we should celebrate. Let's not talk of death and killing right now."

Watching my father's rigid posture relax made me feel relieved to drink. It was very warm inside the great hall, and the bray of drunken men and the madness had no end. Women continued to please the soldiers however they desired, late into the night.

My father patted my hand with his blood-stained palm. Sweat glistened across his forehead. "What a fine daughter I've raised. You will breed strong boys."

"Why Father, I might want to at least finish my meal first," I replied, forcing a smile.

Very quickly, Blaxton's silence came to an end. His voice was urgent. "There is another matter..." His voice boomed loudly throughout the room.

Father looked away from me with a monstrous frustration building up inside. "What matter?" he asked.

"Someone will betray you tonight."

The partiers in the great hall grew silent as the music was hushed. A chorus of panicked voices filled the room.

A soldier screamed, “Don’t listen to him. Everyone in this room is loyal to the general.”

My father slammed his balled, meaty fists on the table, asserting his ferocity, and roared at the top of his lungs. “Traitors, in my army? I’d never believe such a thing.” It was clear my father was highly intoxicated at this point and he just laughed. “You are a fool, Blaxton, or you have drunk too much.”

“I speak the truth,” Blaxton said, with no worry on his face or in his voice whatsoever.

My father laughed again, and in a mocking voice called out, “If there is a traitor in this room—show yourself. Show yourself!”

“Your trust will get you killed,” Blaxton warned. “I know for a fact you will be betrayed tonight.”

My father’s nostrils flared and his voice was hot. There would be nothing that could take us back to the moments before. Blaxton didn’t flinch even when my father looked directly into his black-ringed eyes. I did the same. It was almost like being hypnotized, no matter how much I wanted to tear away; I looked again and again.

“By a Cyan? They don’t have the wit. My house is protected. What right have you to ruin our party with your wild and drunken imaginings? If anything goes wrong, you will be held accountable.”

"The enemy is not planning to storm your walls," Blaxton replied, lowering the glass he drank from. The wine wetting his mouth gave off the effect of blood-tinted lips. "The enemy is already here."

At once, my father gazed at everyone standing on the floor. Terror crept through the room and—by the looks on their faces—none of the party guests knew what might happen next. The revelry died to a whimper, and the players in the orchestra grew pale.

My father looked out into the glittering event, his thoughts, no doubt, grotesque with the paranoia of a madman. The musicians started again at his behest. To and fro the guests danced, my father's eyes scanning the densely packed floor with disgust.

After a few moments, my father leaned over to one of his guards who stood by his side and whispered something into his ear. My father then took a large swallow of his wine and at a sudden wave of his hand, the guards seized the first guest with a violent carelessness.

"Everyone in this party will have to meet with me and answer a few simple questions. I ask that you speak honestly. If an assassin is in this room, I will find him. If I suspect even the tiniest lie, you *will* be hanged from the gatehouse for all to see."

He took another large swig of his wine and gave an evil smile. “Now, until it is your turn to speak with me, pay no attention and dance and drink.”

Wasting no time, the guards shuffled an unwitting guest to stand at my father’s feet.

The first soldier, by the name of Denton Edwards, stood before my father. He had been a loyal fighter for years. He not only fought ruthlessly, but he had been to our house many times as a guest. “This is crazy, sir,” Edwards said, his voice echoing down the hall. “I have been nothing but a loyal and trustworthy soldier. Why are you questioning that?” He swallowed hard. “Would you like me to leave?”

“Well, *go on* then,” my father said.

I couldn’t believe my eyes, I looked around to the others watching with fear as they waited their turns. The orchestra still played without missing a note.

“This is what they want. The Cyan want us at each other’s throats.”

When the soldier was finished talking, my father replied, “That is not the answer I care to hear.”

Edwards sighed. “General, please be reasonable.”

“Hang him first thing in the morning,” my father commanded with zero emotion.

At his guards' shocked looks, my father nodded. His guards took the soldier through the entry doors and out to the cells to await hanging from the gatehouse at first light. My heart skipped, and what I saw did not feel quite real. I pulled on my father's arm, praying he would heed my words. I offered him another glass of wine.

"Drink, Father, please. What about the victory? We should be celebrating. Stop listening to Blaxton. He's just a drunken idiot. No one standing before you plans to kill you. I assure you of this."

He only blinked and didn't sip the wine. His fingers streaked down my face. "I will do what must be done, and I'll hear no more of it."

Then the eldest son of a platoon leader was pushed forward in short order.

"Have you lost your mind?" he asked, pulling away from the soldiers.

"I don't imagine I have..." my father replied with a wave.

Just as quickly, he vanished to be hanged from the gatehouse along with the other soldier recently sentenced to death. Nevertheless, the music still rose off the limestone walls. In fear of reprisal, the guests who were dancing didn't dare to stop. My father was clearly convinced that somehow, with the numbers now steadily dwindling, someone would eventually confess in order to stop this.

He pointed to one of the women, who just shortly before had been riding the cock of a victorious archer. In my father's eyes, she *must* have been the one seeking to betray him. His guards dragged her by the hair, begging for mercy.

"I've done nothing wrong! Please," she cried with tears in her eyes. She clasped her hands and trembled on her knees. "Spare me! Don't be so cruel!"

"I don't know who to believe. Take her, like all of the rest."

And the woman, just as the others, was forced through the entry door to be imprisoned to await her death. Mewling howls whirled in the room as each guest was brought before my father and then summarily seized against their will. Trusted soldiers, commanders, high-ranking officials, women—all were sentenced to hang. The sounds began to soften as less guests leaped up to stand trial before the crazed general.

If one simply stared at the flickering flames on the chandeliers, the dreamlike music, and the half-full glasses and plates on the table, it would appear as though a great bash had come to an end. No, instead my father had to prove a point no matter how many lives it took. Soon enough, the room only had five people left besides the orchestra who still barely played on. Two guards, Blaxton, me, and my father— the general of the Penna.

Very quickly, my father honed in on Blaxton with narrowed eyes. Blaxton hadn't said much since the witch hunt had begun. Not even a twinge of fear crossed his face. He'd led armies thousands of men strong, and facing a gruesome death was merely a fact of life. The man didn't even bother to stand. Instead, he remained seated in his chair.

"You are the one who did this. Your lies," my father shouted. "Their blood will be on your hands."

Expressionless, Blaxton didn't move. "You are nothing but a sick man. A heartless lunatic. I'd rather swing from a rope and be free of you once and for all."

My father craned his neck out further. "So you will..."

My father's words dropped like a hammer on my heart. From where I sat, the guards readied themselves to take Blaxton—their leader—to be hanged from the gatehouse. The orchestra stared into the empty room, afraid to say a word lest they'd be next.

My father glanced at me before savoring a long sip from the glass I'd given him. He smiled at me with a promising, toothy grin. I watched him take another long drink of the wine and smiled back as my heart skipped a few beats.

"You will make the most beautiful breeder, just like your mother."

"I want to be a fighter, not a breeder. I told you this," I answered as I watched him drink the wine.

Suddenly, I watched him stagger back in his chair, swiping something from under his nose. Blood dripped down his red face. My pulse rose as I leaned toward him underneath the gleaming candlelight. His mouth hung agape, and he could not find the words. His breath made flat sucking noises. But no matter how hard he tried, he couldn't get air. He stared into my eyes, clutching at the sparkling silverware and knocking over the wine he'd just drunk.

The wine...

I smiled again. "Did the wine not settle well with you, Father? Or would you like some more poison... I mean... wine?" The evil laced in my voice surprised me.

Realization of who the traitor truly was sank in as he struggled for his final breaths and fell to the floor.

I kneeled, watching him like a cat does a rat. Helpless.

"What would you like me to say, Father? You had it coming. Not only for what you just did—

ordering the deaths of your own people—but I know the truth about how mother died. I did nothing but stand by your side during all of your pillaging and killing innocent Cyans, but you didn't have to kill her," I seethed through closed teeth. I slapped him so hard a red handprint marked his face. "And I told you that I refused to be a breeder and you didn't listen. So I made a deal. I made a deal with your second in command. I kill you—the general—and I get to join the army. Seemed fitting for all you have done. You die, and I profit. Although I would have killed your ruthless ass for free."

He jerked wildly, and his grip softened until his rough hands flopped to his sides. A bitter astonishment spread over his face—he'd been murdered by his daughter. The gurgling sound in his throat made me cover my ears. He reached for me, panting, huffing and unable to cough. The tyrant looked so helpless—like a child who had fallen from a crib. I looked him in the eyes and inhaled a sweet breath of air. It would only be a few more minutes now. The poison seeped through his blood and deep into his bones.

I poured myself a glass of wine, free from poison, as he writhed on the floor and snorted through his nose for air. A tart taste—thick, rich, and acidic—flowed onto my tongue. "Release the prisoners," I commanded as I made eye contact with Blaxton. "And congratulations, Blaxton. You are now the new general."

He simply nodded with a small smile. "Welcome to the Penna army, Alice. I know you will make a great fighter someday."

I FINISHED my story and took a deep breath. I closed my eyes, not wanting to face the condemnation on Rabbit's face. "Not long after, I became a mercenary for the Penna. I believed it was what I was meant to do." I took a deep breath. "So you see, I am a murderer."

Rabbit reached out and grabbed both of my hands in his. He raised them to his lips and kissed the top of each one. For the first time during the whole story, he finally spoke. "Each one of us who fights in battle is a murderer."

I opened my eyes in shock, and rather than seeing judgment, I saw compassion, understanding, and love. Emotions I was not prepared to see, not yet sure if they were truth or illusion.

"No... that is different. I... I am guilty of one of the most evil sins... I am guilty of an awful crime. I murdered my own father."

"We all have killed, my warrior. All for different reasons. Not one of us can judge the actions of men and women in this dark time. You did what you were brought up to do. You were taught not to love, not to show mercy. It was the way of the Penna, and I will never hold that against you."

"Do you think I'm an awful person?" I looked at the feathers on my wrist. "I'm a Penna. I'm ruthless, heartless, cruel."

"Maybe you were. And maybe you still hold those traits deep inside of you. But I'm happy for that. It is what makes you strong. It is what makes me know you can go to battle and come out alive. I don't want you to lose that part of you."

"But you said I should find submission and softness."

"To me. And you have. I love that part of you as well, my dark feather. I love everything and all that you are."

"I killed my father," I whispered.

"Yes, but was he really your father? Did he love you?"

I shook my head. "No, I told you. Penna aren't allowed to love."

"Then he was nothing more than an enemy in battle. He was simply your first kill of many." Rabbit leaned in and kissed me gently on the lips.

"But I hope to end the killing soon. I want to give you so much more. You *deserve* so much more."

"Will that day ever come?"

He sighed. "Maybe not in our lifetime, but someday. It has to. Humanity has to step in sometime and take over."

12

War, death, and more death. It had been going on relentlessly for three weeks now. We had bodies piled up and no time to bury them. I hurried up the windward side of the ridge and felt a striking chill billow against my aching back. In the distance, the sun began to set, beginning the formation of the dark-dusk sky. Instinctively, I raised my arm across my face to shield the white-hot glare from blinding my eyes. Somewhere out there, Rabbit swung his sword into the hearts of our enemy. I drew my hands into my chest, clutching my fingers tightly to try to ease my nerves, wanting desperately to be out in the thick of it.

I wanted to draw my bow and fire off arrows into the men who reveled in the slaughter of innocent people. I didn't expect miracles. In fact, I was prepared for the worst, but secretly I hoped each of Rabbit's men would return in one piece.

The pain deep in my leg was not anywhere as debilitating as standing alone, helpless and far away from the war front. Only a few remained at camp. Most were fighting this war. There I stood; my fingers trembling with anticipation, each passing second stretching like a lifetime, further filling my terrified soul with dread. A small voice within me whispered that he was definitely alive, that he would come as he'd promised. But it would only be drowned out by the far louder one in my head shouting at me to leave and find him myself. Yet the memory of my last spanking and submission to him played heavily in my decision to stay.

Word came back that the battle had been won in our favor. Yes, we had won, but at what cost? I uttered a silent, pleading prayer for just one more glimpse of his face before he was stolen from me. Then a thought came to me. How long could we keep up the fight before Rabbit was eventually killed? Maybe I would die first, or we would die in the same battle. But regardless, we would die. How many soldiers would Cyan sacrifice before realizing this war has no end? There could be no happy ending for us; I knew this to be the truth. Not here, not in this subzero Wonderland.

A sound in the distance brought me back to reality, and I turned to lay my eyes upon a tall figure emerging from the rolling hills of snow and ice. My heart skipped a beat as anticipation filled me, my breath catching in my throat as I waited to see if it would be my true love returning to me, or only my mind playing some terrible trick. Rabbit and his men were marching now— heading right towards me, and I raced down the ridge to finally give my warriors a warm welcome home.

His face was weary, and there were deep circles beneath his dark eyes. He looked very much the part of an exhausted man, rather than that of a weary warrior. He looked broken, almost defeated. And yet, when our eyes met, the pain that had filled his gaze melted away. Neither of us moved for what seemed an eternity, as if both believing the other to be a dream, a mirage conjured up by a tired mind to soothe the tormented soul. He was the first to break the silent stillness that seemed to encompass us like a heavy blanket.

"Alice..." My name bubbled from his lips like the most precious of secrets, his lengthy stride closing the distance between us, and bringing his arms to snatch me up in the warmth of his embrace. The rest of the soldiers marched past us silently, allowing us to reunite in private.

As the days had passed and turned into weeks, fear had planted a seed of doubt within my heart, I had begun to believe Rabbit dead. I did not speak, but the joy I felt shimmered in my eyes, spilling down my cheeks in crystal droplets, soon to be wiped away by dirty fingers from his calloused hands.

“I thought I had lost you.” My voice was barely a whisper above the gentle breeze that blew my hair over one cheek. I gripped what remained of his tattered shirt, fingertips smoothing over ancient scars that littered his pale and battered flesh.

“It was a hard and costly battle, but the thought of breaking your heart kept me alive.” His fingers, stained with blood and dirt, slid over my cheek as his lips met mine in the most tender of kisses. Passionate, fulfilling, perfect. The pain of war, of loss, of defeat—nothing could break his spirit while I still lived. Hope had carried him back to me. When finally our lips parted, there was nothing to be found between us but smiles and warmth, compassion and understanding passing through the depth of our gaze.

“You look exhausted,” I told him, brushing the snowflakes off his brow.

Rabbit pulled me in, kissed me on the

forehead, and answered, "I am alive, and for now, that is all that matters." He pointed at my bandaged leg. "Is it healing any better?" he asked in that intolerably protective tone.

"My leg is fine. It's the best it's going to get," I reassured him. "And you and I both know I am not doing anyone any favors standing on the sidelines. I should have been fighting right beside you."

He looked down at me. Even worse, he looked right through me, utterly perplexed that I'd even make such a statement. "We are not going to debate this."

I bristled from within. Was I just not to have *any* say in the matter? Should I simply spread my legs right this second and resolve myself to being Rabbit's kept concubine?

"Whenever I give you any command, it's your cue to turn everything into a fight. You are a soldier. You take orders. Or do I need to remind you of that with the palm of my hand?"

I took one look at him, eager to get him to listen. "But apparently I am not a soldier. Commanders don't leave their best fighters off the battlefield."

"It is final, there is no use discussing it. You will not be changing my mind," he replied, less politely this time.

"You can't keep me off the line!" I didn't mean

to pick a fight the minute of his return, but I couldn't help myself.

"I will spank you in front of all of these men if you continue to question my decision."

I fell silent and swiftly moved out of the way so he could pass and join the weary soldiers. Rabbit reached for my arm and pulled me close as he headed to his tent. "Come with me."

I looked up into his eyes, trying to read if he was angry. Did he plan on spanking me? "Don't be angry with me."

"I couldn't possibly be angry with you after being apart for so long." He led me to his tent and opened the flap. "But I do need to be alone with you."

In moments, he had removed all his weapons and his bloody, tattered clothes. I rushed off to find a bowl of water so I could clean the death from his body. Walking back into the tent, I found him naked and asleep on his fur pelt.

I debated leaving him and letting him rest, but decided he needed to be free of any memories of the last battle. Dipping the cloth in the water, I began washing the grime off his body with the most tender of touches. He moaned softly but never opened his eyes.

I washed every inch of his body but paused as I reached his sex. Even not aroused, his size seemed daunting. The thought of his cock inside me not only excited me, but it scared me at the same time. I rinsed the cloth and began to rub as gently as I could, trying hard not to wake him. As I washed around his manhood, I watched in fascination as it grew and stiffened.

I jumped and nearly spilled the dish of bloodied water when he asked, “Do you like what you see?”

“I… I didn’t mean to wake you. I was just… I was just cleaning you up.” I placed the bowl down and tried to rise to my feet, but he grabbed hold of my wrist and pulled me close to him.

“Kiss me,” he ordered in a gruff whisper.

I followed his direction gladly. I wanted nothing more than to feel his lips against mine.

“Remove your clothes,” he ordered again.

I stood up and with as much grace as I could muster, removing each item swiftly.

Rabbit stretched out on the bed completely on his back, and rested his hands behind his head, clearly enjoying the display.

“Stand before me.”

I did so without protest.

“Spin, and allow me to see that bottom of yours.”

I did as he asked, turning my back to him.

“Bend over so I can see you on full display.”

I paused for a moment, but did as he asked.

"Spread your cheeks for me. I want to see the bottom hole that I plan to claim."

My heart skipped, but I reached behind me and pulled apart the fleshy mounds of my ass. The cool breeze invading the most intimate of spots sent shivers down my spine. He said nothing for seconds, but it seemed like a lifetime. I remained in position, almost feeling his stare. Juices formed between my silky folds, and I was sure he could indeed see that, as well. I could smell my scent of need and wondered if he could smell it.

I heard the motion of him getting out of bed. I remained in position, determined to stay that way until he gave the command to move. I could hear him rummaging through something, and fought the temptation to glance over.

I jumped slightly when I felt his palm on my ass. "Keep them spread," he directed. A cold liquid touched my hole, and I tensed and nearly let go of my hands. "I want to take you here. I want my cock buried in the depth of your bottom."

My heart beat so hard, I could feel the pulse in my temples. I swallowed back the lump in my throat, trying not to jerk up and run out of the tent. Panic mixed with a forbidden desire to have him do just as he pleased rumbled within me.

He continued to spread the liquid all around

my anus and pressed it past the puckered hole with his finger. He coated every inch of my rosebud, preparing it for entry.

He moved me to the bed and pressed me down to lie on my stomach. "I will be gentle, but this will take some time for you to adjust. I need you to trust me, relax with my touch, and completely give me your submission. If you do so, you will find this highly pleasurable."

I nodded. I couldn't have said anything if I tried. My breathing came in ragged pants, and my body hummed with a sensation I had never known.

He lowered himself over my back and began to softly kiss the side of my neck, my shoulder, my earlobe—each kiss bestowing tingles to my sex. His erection pressed against the crease of my butt.

"I'm scared," I finally admitted.

"I will take care of you. Just breathe and trust me."

"Will this hurt?" I asked, fearful of the unknown. With every spanking of late, Rabbit had been putting his finger and sometimes two inside of me. He warned that he would one day claim my ass, and he was getting me prepared. It seemed that the day of the claiming had finally arrived.

"A little. You will feel a bite of pain as my cock enters you. But as your little hole relaxes, it will allow me better entrance. You just have to relax the best you can." He kissed my neck and nibbled my ear. "But the pleasure I give you will be worth the little bit of pain."

He reached down with his hand and guided his cock to my tight back entrance. Very slowly, and with so much control, he pressed the tip of his dick past the tight ring. He paused so I could get used to the initial shock.

"Relax. Open yourself to me," he purred in my ear, following the words with soft kisses to my neck.

He pushed further, causing me to gasp. The bite, the stretch, the erotic feeling, all became too much. I shook my head. "You are too large for me to accept."

Rabbit whispered in my ear, "Take a deep breath." I did as he asked. "Take another one, and relax your muscles. You need to trust that once I am fully inside you, it will give you pleasure. Submit your fear, your tension, and your body to me."

He reached a hand around my front and found my clit. He circled his finger around, causing me to moan in delight. I focused my attention on the arousal his finger gave me and was able to ease the muscles of my anus. Doing so allowed his cock to press completely into my ass.

"That's it, my love," he praised as he slowly pumped his length in and out. "Let me claim that ass of yours. Let me make you mine."

My bottom hole stretched to impossible levels, but my body heightened with each move of his cock. It was a different type of pleasure than when he gave me an orgasm before, but it was still pleasure.

I had always stood on my own two feet with the strength of ten grown men. I had belonged to no one... until now. Having Rabbit's cock fill my ass and pump in and out gave me a sense of belonging. At that very moment, I was his. I had given myself completely.

"I want to come in your ass," he moaned.

"Yes, yes!"

His gentle thrusts became a little more aggressive. Each push went slightly deeper than before. Tingles in my ass became sparks of ecstasy. My dark channel pulsated around his cock and I screamed out his name.

My sound of pleasure brought on a few more driving thrusts, and Rabbit concluded the conquering with a roar. I could feel his shooting seed fill my hole.

We rested on his bed for quite some time. I listened to his soft snores, knowing he'd used up whatever energy he had left. It took days to recover from battle, though many never had that luxury. I rested my head on his chest, combing my fingers through the black curls that coated it. There was a sense of contentment and safety lying within his arms. But something still bothered me. Would we lose each other in battle?

Irritation bubbled within me at the thought of how Rabbit limited my involvement. No doubt it was because of his fear of losing me; he would die to protect me, this I knew. But I was a soldier. I took pride in being one.

He had declared I could not fight until my leg healed. But it was as healed as it would ever truly be in these conditions. Rabbit was not open to even discussing it further. If I pressed on, I would be disciplined by his hand for sure.

But suffice it to say, it was not over. The last battle, I had complied. But I knew—for the sake of Rabbit—that something more must be done. I remembered something I had once been told. "The deep well is the beginning of all things."

Yes... the well. The Penna had a well... a deep one.

13

The snow of a recent storm came down hard as I rushed to a nearby snowmobile. I launched myself on its frosted seat and drove out into the night. The rich crystalline snow took on an opposite character in the dead of night. It twinkled spectacularly, like a million shining gems, in the sun. But at night, it seemed less magnificent, colder than ever.

Acting on my own was not something I was trained to do. A good soldier followed commands, and there was no way Commander Rabbit White would have approved of me sneaking off into the cloak of the night to attempt to execute what could very well be a suicide mission. No, when or if Rabbit got wind of this, I would surely pay the price. I wouldn't be able to claim I didn't know, because I did. Yes, Rabbit allowed me to fight, but only under his watch and by his side. Tonight, I was alone. And for that, I had no doubt in my mind that my punishment for such an act would be severe. Yet I felt I had no choice. I knew that *if* my plan worked, it could only be done by one person sneaking into Penna territory, and that person would need to be me.

At a distance, I could see the Penna's village, and my former home, smoldering under the smog of dying fires. I stopped the snowmobile, closed my eyes briefly, and took a deep breath to give me courage. Visions of Rabbit's stern stare and warning looks haunted me, and I had to shake them away or lose focus of my mission. I was close enough now that I could walk the remaining distance, and hoped they wouldn't hear my approach.

Eventually, two men appeared on my left. Their voices were loud enough that I could hear their conversation.

"Do you ever wonder why we keep fighting this war? I've heard rumblings from other men that they are tired of the killing, and dying. Do you think we will die before we ever see this end? I don't see us defeating the Cyan as easily as we once thought we would."

"Of course, this whole war is our end. There's word going around that the Penna know our side will fail," one of the thickly muscled soldiers uttered as he walked alongside the other.

"What do you mean?"

"Some believe that if the Cyan continue their attacks like they have, we won't be able to fight them off any—"

The other rebel held out his hand. "Stop. There's something out there," he said.

I kept low, but listened intently. Before the other soldier could respond, however, the snow beneath my boot cracked, and the tiny sound overpowered the pure silence. They had heard me. I knew it. I cursed under my breath, hoping that if I remained completely still, they'd leave me alone. I just needed enough time to get to the well. I could see it. It was so close.

The Penna had built a sturdy defense around the perimeter of the deep well, severely limiting its access to all. Suddenly, the voices I had heard faded away. I didn't even hear so much as a whisper anymore. Turning cautiously, I swept my eyes across the open courtyard. It was almost a straight shot to the deep well.

I recognized its stony circular shape. I quickly rooted through my ratty old satchel. In my hand was poison—the same poison I had used to kill my father. When dissolved in water, the substance would inflict the drinker with a sensation similar to a vice squeezing the heart. I ran as fast as I could toward the Penna's main water supply. Before dropping the poison in the well, I paused. I knew that by doing this, I would kill the entire encampment. My hand trembled over the top of the well.

I closed my eyes to bring me strength. I could do this. I had to do this. The war needed to come to an end. Just let go. Just let the poison go.

I wasn't aware of the assailant until wood made contact with my head with a force so strong I heard my skull rattle. A loud ringing in my ears soon became nothing but darkness.

MY HEAD WAS POUNDING as I opened my eyes with a groan. The room was dark, only lit by the moonlight shining through a high window covered with bars. Looking around as my eyes adjusted, I saw that I was the only one in what I now knew was a cell. I was caught, a captive, a prisoner of war.

Should I say something? Would anybody hear me? It wasn't until I sat squarely on my knees that I realized I was naked. Everything smelled of urine, and I could hear the scurrying of critters hidden in the shadows. I rubbed the large lump on my head where I had been struck. Not sure what to do, I desperately pressed my ear to the stone wall and heard a muffled noise. *Was it screaming?*

I stood, staggering forward a few steps. My ankles and joints felt sore, like I could drop at any moment. With my arms outstretched, it seemed like the blackness had no end.

Someone walked in holding a burning torch, and a stranger in the room spoke. "Our prized archer has returned."

I wrapped my arms around my exposed body the best I could. "Yes," I replied.

The man with the raspy voice walked closer and closer until I could see the depths of his intense brown eyes. Aside from their color, they glistened with a look that sent chills right through my bones. I knew him to be the new general of the Penna. The Penna were on their fourth general since I killed my father, but this one was by far the most ruthless of them all combined.

"Did The Mad Hatter send you here? Or Rabbit White?" the general asked.

"No," I said. "I came of my own accord."

"To kill your own kind? To kill people who have the same blood running through their veins as yours?"

I remained silent.

The man eyed me and kneeled at my side. "I

found this," he said, holding the poison between his index finger and thumb.

I closed my eyes in shame. I still held on to the faintest hope that before I had been knocked unconscious and captured, I had managed to drop the poison in the well. I had clearly failed.

The man grabbed my chin. "I admire you, Alice. Or should I say… mercenary?" he asked with a scorpion grin. "So brave, yet so foolish."

Not once did the ruthless general gawk at my exposed body—his thirst for power overruled any other thirst.

I yanked my chin from his grasp and spat. "Go to hell."

Before I could even prepare, the general pulled back and slapped his hand across my face so hard, I stumbled back in shock.

"Know your place, bitch!" He composed himself and painted a disgusting, vile smile on his face. "If you are a naughty, naughty girl, Daddy will have to step in and teach you a lesson. Would you like that, little girl?"

I glared daggers as my only response.

"Good girl. I didn't think so. I will leave now. You'll need the rest. Tomorrow, you'll no longer be the Cyans' little feathered pet. Tomorrow, I will work you like a fucking dog."

I looked up at him, wanting to attack, to show

he had no control over me, and yet I knew that the sickness I felt in my gut at what Rabbit would endure because of my act was most likely reflected in my eyes. The general spun on his heels with an evil snicker, and I could hear the flat sounds of his footsteps as he exited the chamber. Not too long after he left, I sank down onto the floor, rolled on my back, and closed my eyes as exhaustion took over.

After a too-brief slumber, I heard keys jangle in my chamber door. A soldier violently grabbed my arm and thrust me out of the small stone cell. I collapsed into the snow with my mouth gaping. He tossed a tunic at me. I grabbed it and slipped it quickly over my body, grateful to regain my modesty.

"Walk," the soldier commanded.

I marched forward to the outskirts of the encampment and then beyond. The morning sun shone high over the endless snow. We continued to walk along the icy land until I worried about dehydration and exhaustion. Finally, in the distance, I saw a group of soldiers around what was left of a battle. Dead bodies splayed across the horizon came into view as I made my way to the general himself.

"There is much work to be done here, traitor," the general said. "You see those dead bodies out there? Go bury the men you and your Cyan masters killed." He pointed to the men fallen in the latest skirmish. "Make room for your own when we execute you for treason."

When I didn't move, the soldier escorting me kicked my bad leg, causing me to cry out. "Go!" he shouted. "You heard the general."

"You will do this, Alice. You have two choices. Do it now, as I asked, or do it once we strip you bare. Your choice. But hesitate for a second longer, and you will be nude as you do it," the general spat.

Not wanting to give the men the opportunity to look at what I now considered to belong to Rabbit, I did as the general asked and began digging the hole. Though the subzero temperature would ensure the bodies wouldn't undergo rapid decomposition, the fallen had already become as pale as the snow they lay upon, and as unyielding as the swords they'd wielded. When I draped the stiff arm of a dead soldier around my neck, it felt like I was carrying a heavy block of ice with skin. The corpses were all twice my size, and my shoulders were on fire. I had never been weak, but I found it near impossible to balance the dead soldier's weight. It got heavier with each agonizing step. My sweaty hands lost their grip, and I went tumbling in the snow. I continued picking up the frostbitten bodies, wondering how many I could move before I collapsed.

I glanced over my shoulder and saw a light flicker in the distance. Something, or someone was hiding amongst the ridges. Could it be Rabbit? Would he come looking for me? When he woke and found me missing, would he instantly know what my plan would be?

My answer came in the welcome battle cry of Rabbit's army as they charged the death-infested battleground.

"They're coming! Grab your swords!" the general hollered. He ran to his snowmobile, hooked his hand on a sword, and drove right into the chaos of the fray, a horde of soldiers following suit.

"Spill every drop of their blood!" a Cyan warrior screamed, erupting through the front of the horde. Finally seeing him, I felt overwhelmed when I recognized the man I loved led this attack. He had come for me.

Rabbit swerved past and swung out his sword with surprising speed. In one fell swoop, he hacked through a throng of heads. Rabbit's men pushed through the raging swarm. They pulled their shields forward, forming a surging barricade and then drew their swords. Rabbit struck his sword deep and rapidly pulled back. Blood misted the air as bodies staggered and fell. Endless waves of men sliced through bone in a melee of sharp and jagged swords. Rabbit brought up his arm with a dagger in his fist, and rammed it hard, goring a jagged line down a brute's back. At least a hundred men battled in the hills of snow. Rabbit looked around as his men outnumbered the Penna's dying army. Rabbit drove toward his enemy and the man who had dared capture his woman with vengeance. In a split second, he struck and gouged out the general's eye with little effort as he pushed past him to where I stood.

Rabbit dismounted his snowmobile and stood in front of me. A black rage encompassed his entire being, and a chill ran deep along my spine. The fury of a betrayed man stood before me, and I didn't know what to do or say.

"You came," I eventually said as my legs wobbled beneath me.

The way he looked at me was terrifying. I feared my hero. I dreaded my rescue.

He reached out his hand, and in one smooth action, lifted me up into his seat. He looked into my eyes and patted my leg in reassurance, which allowed me to release the breath I had been holding.

"Thank you—"

"Stop!" he barked. "Do not thank me. Don't say another fucking word until we get to safety."

I nodded my compliance as I didn't dare poke the ferocious bear any further.

I didn't have time to wallow in my shame of upsetting the man I had grown to love, because a surprise attack had me screaming out a warning for Rabbit to watch his back. When Rabbit turned around, the general, with blood gushing out of his eye, brutally tried to stab at him, but missed and slashed along the flesh of his ribs instead. Rabbit bowed slightly, tottering back a few small paces, but quickly shook off the pain. He flipped the knife around and thrust it into the general's thigh. It smashed down so hard it had to have hit the bone. The general spun around and hobbled off into the chaos of battle.

Rabbit mounted his snowmobile while I sat in a stunned daze. He took the handles in his strong grip, trying to hide what had to be a searing pain. A clash of men still hollered as the battle was fought with throaty valor. I slumped against Rabbit's back, my eyes half-open as we charged through the oncoming blizzard and back to our encampment.

14

The shattering roar of hundreds of soldiers fighting to the death could be heard faintly in the setting sun. Effortlessly, Rabbit hopped to the ground. When I tried to mimic the move, I tripped and nearly landed in the snow. He jumped out in front of me and broke my fall. We met eyes until I pulled away.

"I don't know what to say. I went with the intention to poison their water supply," I tried to explain. "It may not have been the wisest move but—"

Rabbit narrowed his eyes. "You'll not say another word!" I had never heard him speak with such venom. The way he looked at me was like a punch to the gut. He was furious. Beyond fury, to a level I had never seen in a man before.

He clasped his hand around my throat and pressed firmly. The shock of his aggression took what little air I had available. A darkness of sorts seemed to blanket his features. "What in the hell were you thinking?" he hissed between clenched teeth. His hand tightened around my throat even more. He could kill me right now if he wanted to. I knew this. I could *feel* this.

"Rabbit," I gasped. "Please let me explain."

"Do not call me Rabbit. You call me *sir* and show me the respect of a commander," he snapped.

His words, his anger, his aggression were far worse of a punishment than I imagined. What I wouldn't do for the biting sting of his hand on my ass instead of this. His fingers tightened around my neck even further until I could barely take in a full breath.

"Sir," I squeaked with very little air.

With his hand tightly around my neck, he pushed me down to my knees so he towered over me. He reached out with his other hand, grabbed a fistful of my hair, and yanked my head back so I had no choice but to stare into his eyes of rage.

"Never! Never again! Do you hear me? Never!" he roared as he yanked my hair so hard my scalp sizzled with pain.

"Yes, sir. Yes, sir."

Rabbit paused for an excruciating moment,

with one hand grasping my hair and the other choking me. Taking a deep breath, he released me, but the fury in his eyes remained.

I needed to remove myself from the situation. Rabbit was pissed, and remaining kneeling before him seemed about as foolish as entering a Penna encampment by myself. "I should go and check on the men. If they are injured, I should—"

He clenched my wrist, and yanked me to standing. "You are in more trouble than you can possibly imagine. It is best you remain quiet and don't do a thing unless I tell you to."

"I was trying to help. I was trying to—"

"Get yourself killed, and kill my men while you do it?" he interrupted. "You left without saying a word. You snuck out of here like a deserter. You disappointed me. You are smarter than that, Alice. You acted like a stupid teenage girl who is crying out for attention. We don't have time for this behavior in the Cyan army. *I* certainly don't have time for this shit."

With tears in my eyes, I threw myself against Rabbit's broad chest which was covered in ice and frozen drops of blood. "I am sorry. I acted impulsively. I don't know why I did it. I just wanted so badly to help, to end this all."

"I should whip you in front of all the men. A lash for every minute you made me fear for your life. Men died and are dying as we speak because of you, Alice! You signed their death warrants with your careless behavior!"

I looked down at the ground and nodded. "I would deserve that, but I hope you take care of matters in private. I deserve the worst kind of punishment. I know that. But please," I looked up at him with tears pouring down my face. "In private, please. Take me in hand as you see fit, but I beg you to spare what dignity I have with these men. I've worked so hard to earn their respect. Please don't make me lose it, even if I actually deserve to."

My shoulders shook with my sobs as I grieved each man who would die because of me. I cried even harder into Rabbit's broad chest when he eventually, and mercifully, held me to him. Such a simple act, and yet the weight of his embrace caused me to release a flood of tears. I cried, I howled, I begged incoherently for forgiveness while he just held me firmly in place.

"I'm so sorry," I finally muttered when I regained some control in my complete meltdown. "I know I don't deserve you to forgive me, since I did put so many lives at risk. But please, Rabbit. Please, forgive me." I sniffed and swiped away my tears as I pulled back just enough to look into his eyes as he looked down at me. "I am so sorry. Never again. I will never again act alone."

"I thought I'd lost you," Rabbit whispered as he stroked my hair. His voice softened. "I feared I wouldn't reach you in time."

I didn't know until that minute how badly I needed a sign of his love. I could no longer hold back the sobs I believed I had regained control of and cried again, releasing my pain, my fear, and my shame even more. Would I ever stop? Would I ever be free of the darkness inside of me?

After a few moments, I pulled back and swiped at my tears once more, remembering that Rabbit was injured. I looked down as he lifted his tunic. Expecting to see a deep gash at the very least, and a gaping, jagged wound at the worst, I was surprised to see a thin red line along his side. Though it was oozing blood, it wasn't going to kill him. However, from the look in his eyes, I might not be so lucky

"I will be fine. It's superficial at best." He glared at me. "After I am finished with you, my wound will seem minimal compared to your discomfort." He wrapped his arms around me tightly and kissed the top of my head. "You understand a punishment is due? Not a tantalizing game of submission, but a true punishment."

I nodded, trembling against his hard torso. He took a deep breath and let me go.

"Now, go get cleaned up and settle in for the night," he whispered in my ear. I didn't want to let him go. As I walked to enter the tent, I looked back and saw Rabbit getting back on his snowmobile.

"You're leaving now?" I asked, my cheeks wet from tears.

"I will be back before morning. I need to make sure all my men return. The battle is not over yet." He gave a reassuring smile and then a glare. "When I return, be waiting for your punishment."

I wiped my puffy eyes with the back of my hand. Rabbit's snowmobile revved loudly before taking off toward the enemy—and possible death—again. This was all because of me, and the shame I felt brought on a new wave of tears. What was wrong with me? Crying? Penna don't cry! Penna don't care! Penna don't love. And yet… I was doing all three.

He summoned me the next morning, and I arrived with a heavy heart. I had been up all night as his disappointment in me broke my spirit. He was dressed down as much as he could be with the cold temperatures even inside the tent; a belted tunic, undershirt, and trousers in the palest of brown tones. As soon as I arrived, he gestured for me to enter fully—but he didn't turn to face me. I stopped a few feet away after doing as I was bid. Hesitation tangled at my feet before I finally drew the courage to speak.

"Rabbit?"

"Alice." He finally turned to face me, but his expression was somber—verging on grim. "The mess you made is cleaned up... for now."

"My apologies, sir. It will not happen again." I ducked my head repentantly and stared at my hands, folded as they were in front of me.

"*I* will see that it doesn't."

"Yes, sir."

The silence that hung after my words was painful, and I fought the urge to lift my head and look upon his face. It was only when he closed the distance between us, and touched my chin with his fingers, that I had no choice but to look into his dissatisfied expression.

"I should take you outside and spank you in front of all the men. I should show them what happens to foolish girls. If you act like a reckless child, I should treat you like one."

My heart stopped, and I had the sudden urge to vomit. "Please, no." I knew I would never regain the men's respect if that were to happen. That first time... the day I had wandered into their camp had been different. Yes, Rabbit had ordered me stripped, had spanked my bare ass, but things had changed... we had changed. The thought of having my nude bottom exposed again to all their lurking eyes made my body break out in a cold sweat.

"It is lucky for you that they are under the belief that I ordered the espionage, and you were only acting on command." He began to pace the room. "Because of that, your punishment will be for my eyes only."

A wave of relief washed over me. "Thank you," I barely whispered. I wanted desperately to cry and to beg him just to hold me. I wanted his loving touch so much that it physically hurt. I had endured injuries in battle. I had felt the burning slice of a blade against my skin, and yet nothing made me ache as much as I did knowing how deeply I'd disappointed this man.

He didn't so much as smile. He stopped pacing and stood before me again. My breath caught in my chest, and I felt terribly faint as my fingers tightened in the folds of my tunic, desperate to clutch something, anything at all, for support.

"This spanking is not going to be like the others. This is a punishment. This will hurt."

"Yes, sir." The words spilled out, breathless and aching. I gathered the courage to look up and the tears that had built in my eyes ultimately dared to stream forth. "I am sorry."

"Get undressed and lie across my bed on your stomach." The command came with force, and I uttered a small moan of misery.

"Now."

I shuddered and quickly followed the order as he demanded. I could smell the scent of fur from the pelt on his bed becoming stronger as it became soaked with the tears I couldn't hold back. The disappointment in his voice, the way he looked at me, all created the worst type of punishment before the first blow even came. I could feel my breath and hear the quivering of it all the more keenly.

It felt like an eternity before his hand came to rest on the back of my head. He stroked his fingers through my hair, and I was aware he was kneeling near me, but only on one knee.

"You are a good girl, Alice. Your submission to this punishment will work in your favor."

He withdrew his hand and stood. I could hear him moving away, could imagine him turning his back to me. I started to cry again, and the weight of his silence only made it worse.

"I will not be using my hand this time. Leather to your backside should teach you a good lesson for your recklessness."

My stomach sank, and yet a sexual thrill pulsed in my pussy. The confusion of the two senses made my head spin. I glanced over my shoulder, took a moment to study him, and was struck by the severity of the leather strap in his hand. I nervously wet my lips and placed my face against the pelt.

I heard the leather before I felt it. Fire erupted on my skin with the first searing whip, and I cried out with the surprise of the sting.

"I give orders as your commander, but more importantly as a man who loves you," he said as he continued to tan my hide with the leather.

"I belong in battle. I'm not a fragile vase that needs to be handled gently," I protested hotly. "If I must be spanked to fight, then so be it."

Rabbit rewarded my outburst with several more whips of the strap. I howled with the last one as the burn blazed from the globes of my ass to my upper thighs.

"You are being disobedient," he pointed out with a cool edge to his tone. He continued to whip as he lectured. "I will punish the disobedience right out of you."

I regretted my statement as the punishment continued on. Leather against flesh, tears against fur, and sweat beading all over. Never had Rabbit been so harsh with me.

"Perhaps you did not hear me when I told you that you were far too injured to fight. Perhaps you didn't hear me when I told you to remain at camp until directed otherwise."

The options were offered, but I knew the only answer. I groaned and his fiery lashes continued.

"In either case, you will follow my orders, or else. You will never put your life at risk without my knowledge of you doing so. And if you disobey me again, the next punishment will be for *all* to see." His voice dropped a little, a threat lingering in the undertones.

He stopped the spanking, and I took a shaky breath, grateful the punishment had come to an end. Although the assault to my backside was over, I remained in position until Rabbit told me otherwise. I worried that any act which did not drip with submission, would earn me more of a whipping.

"Let me ask you something," he began. His touch on my ass startled me, but I moaned when he gently caressed my seared flesh. "When you went to that camp, were you prepared to die? Did you think you would die?"

I nodded against the fur. "Yes, sir."

"For the sake of the Cyans? For the sake of the war?"

I nodded again. "Yes, sir."

He continued to caress my bottom, gently

squeezing my punished flesh. "Did you think of me? Of what I would do or feel?"

I swallowed hard. What would I say to that question? The truth? "In the beginning, I did. I knew I would be punished for what I was doing… if I survived the mission."

"And did you fear that punishment?"

"I…"

"Did the thought of my wrath even make you falter?" he asked while squeezing a cheek of my ass so hard, I whimpered in pain.

"No, sir. I did not fear you. I thought about the punishment and was prepared to take it in order to poison the camp. In my eyes, it would have been worth it."

"Worth the punishment?"

"Yes, sir."

"Well then, it is my job right now to make sure you *learn* to fear a true punishment from me." He swatted my bottom hard with his hand and then swatted me again even harder. "After this is over, you will most certainly fear my wrath if you are ever so foolish as to earn another."

I moaned in response and gripped the fur in anticipation of a punishment that was far from over.

"You will never cause me such agonizing fear again. You are mine, and are no longer allowed to make decisions that could affect us both without my involvement. You are mine!"

Instantly, fire erupted on my exposed bottom once again. Over and over, the lash came crashing down. Each whip of the leather against my upturned ass made me cry out. I didn't hold back at all, and could not care less that all the soldiers could hear my cries. They knew Rabbit was not a man to cross, and they all knew I belonged to him. I'm sure it didn't surprise them one bit that Rabbit exuded dominance in all ways.

I thought the first round of my spanking had been awful, but nothing compared to the severity of the whipping I was receiving now. Each strike of the leather had me flinching and writhing in pain. It burned, it throbbed, it stung, and I could do nothing more than helplessly lie there and take it. And when I foolishly kicked up my legs, trying to fight off the foray of blows, I was rewarded with the belt whipping my legs back down into submission.

"Rabbit! No more," I begged. "It hurts! I can't!"

As if I were mute, and my cries could not be heard, Rabbit continued. Every single inch of my ass had met with the leather of the belt repeatedly.

Thirty lashes.

Forty.

I lost count.

"Rabbit! No more! I beg you! No more!" My

pain was uncontrollable and a sense of panic set in that I would indeed die from the pain erupting on my rear. And yet, Rabbit continued.

"Do you fear my punishment now?" He brought the leather down even harder.

"Yes! Oh! Yes! I will never do something to deserve this again! I swear! Please..."

"Will you think of me? Think of how I would feel? Will you take pause enough and remember this day before you ever make a rash decision again? Will you fear my wrath now if you ever earn a punishment of this nature?"

Tears cascaded from my eyes, and I thickly uttered my tearful apology. "Yes, sir. I understand. I-I won't put you through that again. I let my foolish pride get in the way of reason. I'm sorry, I'm so, so sorry, I..."

The punishment ended abruptly, and I felt his arms take hold of me. He guided me up effortlessly, placed me in his lap, and kissed away the tears that glazed my cheeks as I hiccupped and winced against the pain.

"I hope to never have to take you to task in such a way again," he whispered, stroking my hair as I cuddled into his neck. "I know I was hard on you." He kissed the top of my head. "I had no choice. I had to make sure you would never do this again. I needed to make sure that the next time your impulsive nature takes over, you will at least take pause."

"It hurt," I whimpered as I continued to cry.

"And it pains me that I had to do that. But, Alice, I was so scared. I was terrified that I would never get to see you again, and I swore that if I did get to see you again, I would tame the wild beast in you to ensure I would never lose you again. I would make damn sure you would never try to sacrifice yourself again."

I pulled away and looked into his eyes that were glistening with tears. The pain on his face stabbed my heart and caused more pain than the hot throbbing on my ass.

"I was scared, too. I have never felt fear before. But when it dawned on me that I wouldn't see you again, I actually felt fear for the first time in my life." I sniffled and still shook from all the sobs that took over my body. "I don't ever want to feel that fear again."

"I love you, Alice. God, if you only could feel how much I do." He held me close and allowed my body to recover some more before asking, "Do you feel I was too harsh on you?"

"Yes, you were harsh," I mumbled against his chest. My ass sizzled in pain, and I knew I would be feeling the burn for hours if not days to come. "But the worst part is how ashamed I am for letting you down."

"Release the shame. The discipline has erased all your wrongdoing, and it has set us right again. Please no longer feel ashamed." He kissed me several more times as he rubbed my back gently. "It's over. This awful nightmare is over."

"So you forgive me?" I asked.

"Yes, of course I do. There is nothing you can do, Alice, that I would not forgive. You are mine, and I am yours. I may have to continue to tame that stubborn and wild streak in you." He chuckled lightly. "And I will tame you, make no mistake. But I will always forgive, and I will always love."

I sat there on his lap, my ass burning as hot as the sun, and yet as I regained my composure, I had never felt so loved. I had just been given the whipping of a lifetime, but now the negativity melted away in his arms. The paradox of punishment and love surprised me, but at the same time, pleased me.

He pulled my face away from him so I was looking into his eyes. "I cannot express the power of my love for you. It stabs at my heart like a fucking dagger." He tightened his arms around me and placed a gentle kiss on my chapped lips. "I cannot stand another day with you not being fully mine."

“Then make me yours, Rabbit. Please,” I begged. “Let us not wait until marriage. We may not live until that day.”

He palmed my pussy and dipped his finger past the folds. Surprised by how a thrashing from Rabbit could cause such wetness, I could only moan in delight.

“Your virtue…” Rabbit resisted in word, but his hand continued to fondle my sex.

“Yes, my virtue belongs to you. It is my gift I freely give to you.” I didn’t wait for a response but slid from his lap, pulling him up as I frantically removed his clothes in a whirlwind of yanks and pulls before he could change his mind.

“Alice, I want to make you my bride.” His dark eyes met mine. “I want to be your husband.”

“Yes. In time, we will. But we are on this brutal land for what could be our lifetime. I don’t want to die not knowing what it feels like to have you deep inside of me. What if I had died rather than just been captured? I would have died with virtue, but without the knowledge of the deepest connection.”

He stared in silence as if he were considering my words.

I pressed on. “Tonight may be the only night we have. There may never be another. I can’t bear leaving Wonderland without feeling what it would be like to make love to you. Or worse… if you were to leave me before claiming me fully. I belong to you. My heart is yours and always will be. My soul is yours." I paused to see if I was getting my point across. "I respect your belief and understand why you feel that way, but you once said that we live in dark times. Don't you think we have to accept that fact and live for the moment?"

It was as if those words shattered his wall of opposition. He pressed me down to sit on the bed, fire burning in his eyes. Soon, he stood naked before me and pushed his hard cock past my lips. He began to thrust his hips back and forth as he fucked my mouth with vigor. I opened wider, struggling to not gag against the size pressing to the back of my throat. Over and over he pressed.

"Do not close your eyes. Look at me fully," he commanded.

I opened my eyes and stared into the darkness of his as he continued to possess my mouth.

"If I take you, in my eyes you will be my bride."

I nodded while I sucked harder.

"The moment my seed fills your pussy, I will be your husband."

I nodded again.

"Do we agree on my terms?"

I nodded as tears streamed down my face.

He removed his cock from my mouth, lowered me to my back, and lay on top of me. His weight, his closeness, and his heat made my body beg to be taken.

He paused and took a deep breath. Any sign of animalistic desire soon became replaced with a soft and gentle kiss. His tongue danced with mine with the most delicate touch. His hand caressed my face as he slowly gyrated his dick against my moist clit. The tip of his cock made small circles, pulling the sexual need from my body. He kissed his way down to my breasts, sucking on my hard nipple, moaning around the softness. He devoured my flesh with his mouth as if my breast gave him life. The wetness of his tongue circling the nipple caused my body to burn with an even higher state of arousal. An inferno blazed inside my core.

He pulled away and looked into my eyes. A connection formed between our stare that neither of us wanted to break. "I love you," he whispered.

"As I love you."

He positioned his body so his hardness rested against my wetness. "Alice, do you take me to be your husband, swearing to love and honor me for all eternity?"

I swallowed hard before nodding. "I do." My voice shook slightly.

Rabbit kissed me deeply as he pressed the tip of his cock to my virginal entrance, not yet pressing in.

"Do you, Rabbit, take me to be your wife, to protect and honor me through the years?" I asked, playing along in his romantic game.

"I do," Rabbit responded, kissing me even deeper. "I now pronounce us, husband and wife," he declared, his own voice beginning to shake. "May we live long, prosper, and be fruitful in whatever land our journeys take us. You and I are married by my declaration. I have deemed it so under God, in the name of our love. We are now joined for all eternity." Smiling slightly, he added, "We may now kiss."

Kissing me again, Rabbit pressed his cock into my tight hole in one fluid motion. He paused, a slight look of worry crossing his face before he swept in and pressed his lips firmly against mine. Gently but firmly, he pushed his cock further, breaking the virginal barrier.

I tensed for a moment, taking in the pain of the intrusion. He soothed me with gentle kisses and hushed words. He paused so I could adjust to the size of his girth buried inside me. When the discomfort diminished, I began to move my hips in a silent plea for more.

In and out, Rabbit slowly eased his cock past my silky folds. My moans blended with his, just as our passion united. My pussy stretched with each thrust of his hips, sending jolts of electricity to my core. I could feel the orgasm building at a speed that threatened to take my breath away.

"Rabbit," I gasped, clinging to his back with my nails.

He continued to drive deeper and harder, picking up the pace as my orgasm grew nearer.

"Rabbit," I gasped again, arching my back to meet his ramming cock.

The sound of his balls slapping against my wet pussy tantalized my senses. I could smell the musky scent of my arousal. My punished ass moved against the fur, reminding me of my new husband who could most certainly take me in hand. My body radiated with life, and the building orgasm exploded.

Again, not caring who could hear outside the tent, I screamed in wild abandon. Rabbit continued to pound his cock into me at a frenzied pace until he too called out my name in a guttural moan. He released his seed in me as my orgasm subsided.

Breathing heavily, we both held each other in silence. United and married by love.

15

We stepped out of the tent, the soldiers were going about their duties as usual. The sun was just touching the western edge of the icy land, turning the snow pink and lavender with its slowly failing rays. A cool breeze whispered around, promising a new snowstorm for the evening. We had spent the entire day making love, sharing stories of our past, laughing, and for the first time in my entire life, planning and daydreaming about our future. It was our rumbling stomachs that forced us to finally leave our tent, and Rabbit decided he wanted all to know of our wonderful news.

As we approached the middle of camp, the men moved apart and nodded their greeting. I slowly moved forward, my nerves heightened.

Rabbit led the way, his face lighting up as he reached for my hand.

"Don't be nervous. I'm proud to announce you as my wife," he whispered in my ear. I smiled, blushing as we stood in the middle of camp.

As silence fell around us, Rabbit waited for everyone to gather. The soldiers could see he would make an announcement. "I would like to inform my fellow soldiers that I had the honor of making Alice my wife. Please acknowledge and show her your respect as I know you will. Tonight, we celebrate!"

Ovation rang out amongst the men as Rabbit pulled back slightly and looked into my eyes again. "You are even more beautiful today, now that you stand here as my wife," he whispered, before leaning forward for another kiss. The cheers of the men grew even louder.

Finally pulling back, he turned and stood alongside me, facing the men. Taking my hand, he pulled me close and slid his arm around me. Then, with deliberate care, he led me through the cheering men to accept their wishes for the future.

Rabbit and I remained side by side for most of the evening, the only exception being when he would get pulled away by a soldier offering advice when it came to women. As the evening darkened and the stars came out, everyone slowly finished the jovial talk and left to return to their tents, leaving Rabbit and me alone in the frosty night.

"This icy land brought us together," he said as he wrapped an arm around my shoulder.

I nodded. "Yes."

"You are so beautiful in the glow of our love, but I still remember how beautiful you were the first time I saw you."

I laughed. "I was covered in snow, blood, and my filthy hair was knotted and matted, hardly beautiful for any woman."

"It was the fire in your eyes and your spirited courage that made you stunning then. It is not looks, but your heart and spirit that make you beautiful to me. I was hooked the minute I saw you."

"So you had me chained? Naked?" I asked as I playfully shoved him in the arm.

"I had to gain the upper hand somehow. Trust me, your eyes and the way you looked at me were more powerful than any weapon you could have ever used. I was hypnotized."

I huffed. "Is that why it was so easy for me to kick your ass when you were testing my abilities?" I giggled.

Rabbit chuckled. "I let you win."

"You did not! I surprised you."

He smiled a large, toothy grin. "All right, you

kicked my ass. And yes, you surprised me. I had no idea that such a fighter could be inside such a beautiful woman. I can't wait to have children with you, for no doubt they will be just as wonderful as you."

My smile faded and I looked up to the starry sky. "We can't have children. I'm mutated, remember?" The thought of never being able to have his children broke my heart. But this wasn't a gift I could give him.

"Why the hell not? And don't ever call yourself a mutant again unless you want another taste of my leather."

"But I am," I insisted as tears filled my eyes. "The cDermo-1 runs through my veins and, therefore, would run through any baby's I brought into Wonderland."

"So? What is so awful about that?" He reached for my wrist and ran his fingertips along the edges of the feathers softly. "I like your feathers. I don't like that they were forced upon you, nor the beliefs behind the Penna, but they do serve a good purpose. You never have to worry about freezing to death. You don't feel the bitter cold as I do." He brought my wrist to his lips and gently kissed the feathers. "I love that you can give the gift of warmth to our children."

I started to sob as all the insecurities, all the

hate of my body, all the deep disgust of what I thought I was—a mutant—left my body. With Rabbit's simple and honest words, he freed me from a darkness I had carried my entire life. He loved me. He loved every inch of who I was, both inside and out. He allowed me to be strong, and also allowed me to be weak. He loved the blood-stained, dirty soldier just as much as he loved the jeweled and gowned woman. He embraced me. He loved me... a Penna. He loved me... his dark feather.

Rabbit led me back to his tent as the stars glinted in the deep indigo vault of the heavens. We walked into his tent, which would now be ours. Gently, he guided me to the bed. I slipped out of my clothing and stood alongside him, completely nude, as he did the same. It was as if we had done this so many times in how natural we were. My body, my soul, and my heart now belonged to him.

Lowering me onto the bed, Rabbit reached for my wrist and placed soft kisses along the feathers. When he was done with one wrist, he grabbed my other wrist and kissed there, as well. Mumbling against the kiss, he whispered, "So exotic, so sexy," he moaned, "my dark feather. Never doubt for one minute how beautiful I feel they make you."

Still new to the art of making love, I tentatively lowered my hand to his hard cock and stroked it as he licked along the edges of my feathers. He eventually made his way, one delicate kiss at a time, to my pert nipple and took it into his mouth, rolling it along his tongue, and squeezing it between his lips. Arching my back, closing my eyes, I moaned in pleasure, almost forgetting that I had his large cock held firmly in my hand. The silky smoothness of his dick as it flexed in my palm, brought me back to the now.

I wanted him.

I wanted him this very second.

Now.

Rabbit continued to suck my breast, then moved to the other to give it equal attention. Lowering his hand to my mound, damp with my own arousal, he dipped a finger to my clit and applied pressure as he roused an overwhelming longing that had me gasping for air. Moving from my clit, he pressed his fingers past my silky folds and pushed one, then two, digits into my sex. I forced my hips up to drive them inside my pussy even deeper. They weren't enough. I wanted to feel the small bite of pain as his cock stretched me as he claimed what was now his. I wanted to feel him so bad that the hunger changed who I was.

I was an animal.

I was a hunter in search of its prey.

I was a woman who needed to be fucked hard

by her man.

Not being able to hold back the fever that scorched me, I begged, "Please, Rabbit. Please..."

"Please what?" he asked as he danced his fingers inside of my core. "Say it, Alice. Tell me what you want."

"I want you," I panted, desperately wanting to feel the orgasm that rested just beneath the surface, begging to be set free. But I needed Rabbit's cock to make that happen.

"Say it, Alice. Say what you really feel."

"Fuck me!" I blurted out as a moan followed my command. "I want you to fuck me hard, and make me remember the feeling between my legs for days. Make me sting. Make me hurt. Fuck! Fuck me!" I was absolutely desperate at this point as his fingers hit a spot inside my pussy that had me gyrating uncontrollably. I needed more! I needed him so bad that I could have lost my mind in wild thirst for more if he didn't mount me and take me right then.

Merciful as he was, he did just as I needed. Feeling his weight on top of me, I was soon rewarded when his cock pressed up against my opening, and easily slid in with the aid of my wetness. Wrapping my legs around him, I held on in fear that I would cede complete control over to the lust.

I was so hungry.

I had such a craving and an urge that only he could quench.

And with a forceful shove of his hips, he drove his thick cock all the way in, claiming me completely. Yes, yes, yes… I was his. I was finally his.

In and out, he thrust, deeper and deeper with each one. My moans blended with his as our bodies merged as one. He was my commander, and my body would forever be his to lead, to master, to conquer.

"So fucking good," he growled as he powered into me, his muscles taut, his eyes glazed over. "Come for me," he groaned. "Come for me."

As if I needed the command, like a dutiful soldier, I did just as he ordered. A wave of warmth that had been resting on the cliff since he took my nipple into his mouth finally released. Pure carnality shook through my body as I screamed out his name… my husband's name. Moaning with each pulsation of decadence that attacked my pussy, I truly melted into an abyss of sexual heaven. With a few more thrusts, Rabbit joined in with the pleasurable moans, and he too joined me in our own utopian paradise.

After a few moments of deep breaths on both of our parts, he looked deep into my eyes. "On this day, I make a promise to you. We will end this war in peace. Somehow, some way, we will reclaim our lives in peace. You and I will stop the fight. I am ready for calm. I am ready for stillness. But above all, I am ready for a life with you."

"And then what?" I asked warmly, as I positioned my body so I could snuggle on his chest. "All we know is war. What will we do if we don't have to get up and battle every day?"

He pulled me close to him tighter and thought for some time before speaking. "Go back to Danis and have babies. Live a simple life. Somehow figure out how to better survive this harsh land and make it better for the next generation. I want more for our children. But basically I want us to be bored out of our minds."

I smiled at such a wonderful thought, and felt like I had been lit up from the inside by a ray of sunlight breaking through my internal storm. Wiggling on top of Rabbit, I kissed him firmly on the lips. "We will never be bored. Adventure is in our soul, I will not let us become soulless."

He chuckled. "Life with my warrior will be full of adventure, I have no doubt."

"You would have it no other way," I teased, embracing him with my whole body.

Rabbit laughed before tumbling me over and pinning me down. Gently, he kissed along my jaw.

"You are right; I would have it no other way. I promise you, Alice. I promise you that we will end this war side by side. But it will end."

Our perfect bubble popped with the sound of shouts and chaos erupting outside. The sound parted and died away. Footsteps came closer, and the door of the tent was swept aside to reveal a soldier. Rabbit and I inhaled sharply as I scrambled to conceal my body.

Rabbit stepped forward in fury, trying to block me with his large frame. "How dare you just storm into my tent! Never enter my—"

"Forgive me, sir. But the scout has just arrived and warned that an army of a hundred are marching our way. A surprise attack, no doubt." The soldier looked down at the ground as I quickly dressed. "The Penna will be here by dawn if we don't head them off."

Rabbit glanced over at me with regret in his eyes before turning back to the soldier. "Prepare the men," he ordered.

The night passed in a whirling blur as the army prepared to meet the Penna head on. Dawn came too soon, and the snow turned a shade of rose in the new light. As I exited the tent, Rabbit approached me gravely. "Would you stay back if I asked you as your husband, not your commander?"

"Would you ask me to stay back as your best archer and not your wife?"

Rabbit frowned. "No."

I nodded and mounted my snowmobile. "Then I think you know the answer," I said with a warm and loving smile. I started my engine and gave him a reassuring look, silently promising him that all would be well. "We have a battle to win, my love," I declared before turning my snowmobile and heading toward the enemy.

Rabbit caught up to me on his own machine and grabbed hold of my handles, causing both of us to stop. "I would like a kiss from my bride before we leave." He swatted the side of my bottom and added, "And I am the commander. I declare when we leave for battle."

"Yes, sir," I said with a wink.

I smiled as my heart soared with love. I leaned in and met his lips with mine. Offering a last smile, and a kiss upon his cheek, I turned to make my way toward the battle.

My heart was calm, my mind at peace. I could never have the sweet, gentle life of a wife and mother until this war was over. But I believed that we could end it. We were close. We were so very close. And until the white flag was flown above the equally white landscape, I would fight beside my commander and my husband.

EPILOGUE

Five more years of bloody battles ensued. So many died, and so many paid the price for... for what? If you asked the soldiers why we were fighting, many could not clearly answer that question. Hate? Vengeance? Power? The need for blue-green algae? Maybe all of the above, but the main question that had loomed in all of our minds was: why? And that question weighed heavy on all of our souls until finally the day came when enough of the mercenaries, soldiers, commanders, killers alike—on both sides—had had enough. We needed to unite—both Penna and Cyan—to defeat Death before he won the battle over all. So, like Rabbit had predicted, the white flag finally rose on both sides, and a truce had been negotiated.

The day on which the peace talks came to an

end, and The Mad Hatter and the general for the Penna signed a declaration for peace and unity, icy Wonderland celebrated as one. The war was over.

It was also on this momentous day that Rabbit and I celebrated our own victory. After five long years in battle as husband and wife, fighting side by side, we could finally stop. And we could finally have what we had always wanted—a future.

The day the declaration for peace was signed, we welcomed our little baby boy, Cheshire Penna White, into Wonderland. He was born a Cyan but would always have a bit of Penna inside of him. And though Wonderland was nothing more than a large ball of ice, I was able to give him the greatest gift of life.

Feathers.

Warmth.

"He's perfect, Alice," Rabbit said as he swiped my sweaty hair from my forehead and wrapped his arm around my tired body. I snuggled into his embrace as I held my baby boy, admiring how he looked in his first moments of life.

"He is. He has feathers like we predicted." I stroked my fingers softly against the white fluff of feathers that rested on his shoulders and ran along his spine. "He's our perfect angel."

"Well look what we have here," The Mad Hatter said as he knocked on the door just before he entered the room. "Cousin, you just gave birth to a new mighty warrior for the Cyan." He walked up and patted Rabbit on the back. "Too bad that, as of today, it looks like the war with the Penna is over." The Mad Hatter leaned down and kissed me softly on the forehead. "How is mother holding up?"

"I'm absolutely perfect. Better than perfect," I gushed as a happiness I never knew possible filled my soul with warmth. "Meet Cheshire Penna White."

"Yes, quite a fine man you have on your hands," The Mad Hatter said with a beaming smile.

Rabbit looked up at him with pride exuding from every ounce of his being. "Did you sign the declaration? Was there any resistance?"

"Everyone signed and shook hands as men of our word. It's over. I didn't think I would see this day come in my lifetime, but I can finally say that the war with the Penna is over." The Mad Hatter leaned in and touched the feathers on the baby's shoulder. "Stunning. What a magnificent being he is. Maybe this little man will be our next Cyan leader someday."

"What do we need a leader for if we are no longer at war?" I asked, still not able to take my eyes off my son. I never believed that you could actually *see* peace, until I watched my baby boy breathe deeply in his sleep.

"To lead us in our new battle. The battle of our lifetime is still ahead of us," The Mad Hatter informed.

"How so?" I asked.

"When we signed the declaration of peace, we also signed a declaration of war."

Rabbit looked up in shock. "War? What happened?" All the ease, comfort and satisfaction had left him instantly, and his warrior pose resumed. "The Penna? Did they betray us?"

The Mad Hatter shook his head. "The Penna and the Cyan have signed a declaration of war against the Wonderland. We have agreed to work together to find a way to master this planet before it masters us. There is so much we can still do to utilize the blue-green algae that both the Penna and Cyan can agree on. We all want the best for mankind, and have agreed to work together on that one purpose. And it's quite possible that we may utilize the cDermo-1 to help us battle the freezing Wonderland. I think the Cyan need to admit that the Penna may have been right in regards to that. Without it, we may all eventually freeze to death. The temperature of Wonderland keeps dropping."

I looked at Rabbit with a smile and said, "It appears that your son and I may not be the only ones in this family with feathers on our skin." I giggled. "I won't be your dark feather anymore if we are all the same."

He leaned in and kissed me on the lips before saying, "You will always be my dark feather. Nothing will ever take away that fact." Rabbit smiled and once again, a calm and stillness washed over him as he watched baby Cheshire sleep in my arms.

The Mad Hatter touched the baby's hand. "This little guy is the next generation. I have no doubt he can lead this fucked up Wonderland back to civilization. Not just survival like we do now, but true advancement. He will be part of creating a new empire. An empire of evolvement that can thrive with the ice rather than be at its mercy." The Mad Hatter smiled when Cheshire stirred a little and opened his eyes to stare up at him. "I have no doubt in my mind. This little boy will master the ice."

"Master the ice," I whispered, liking the sound of that. I silently vowed in that moment that his father and I would give our beautiful boy the tools to do so, and we wouldn't stop until he did.

"Yes. You are right, Mad Hatter. My son will be the perfect soldier for such a mission."

Yes, my little angel would make the perfect soldier in this new war. He had the best of the

Penna, and the best of the Cyan inside of him. Cheshire was the first good thing that came from this war. He symbolized peace, unity and progression. I looked up into the eyes of the man I loved, and saw that he too felt the same. Rabbit leaned toward me and gently kissed my lips as he held baby Cheshire's hand lightly. It was time we started the next siege. It was over, and yet, it had just begun. We were soldiers, and would forever fight the war... together.

And They Lived Happily Ever After...

Are you ready read another dark fairytale?
The Truth About Cinder is next!

The evil lies little girls are told...

There are hushed whispers about a wicked and decadent place known as the Palace of Lazar. A prince with insatiable tastes and the women who cater to it all. Feasts of pleasure, lust, and forbidden acts... all submitting to the sensual allure of the Harem.

But behind its bejeweled façade of luxury and pleasure lies a haunting and evil truth. A dark and perverse world that only the strong can survive.

A truth Cinder is about to learn when her fairytale dreams become twisted into a macabre masquerade of dancing vices.

Will she succumb to the demands of her current story, or cling to her fairytale ending?

ABOUT THE AUTHOR

Alta Hensley is a USA TODAY bestselling author of hot, dark and dirty romance. She is also an Amazon Top 100 bestselling author. Being a multi-published author in the romance genre, Alta is known for her dark, gritty alpha heroes, sometimes sweet love stories, hot eroticism, and engaging tales of the constant struggle between dominance and submission.

Check out Alta Hensley:
Website: www.altahensley.com
Facebook: facebook.com/AltaHensleyAuthor
Twitter: twitter.com/AltaHensley
Instagram: instagram.com/altahensley
Amazon: amazon.com/Alta-Hensley
BookBub: bookbub.com/authors/alta-hensley
Sign up for Alta's Newsletter: readerlinks.com/l/727720/nl

ALSO BY ALTA HENSLEY

Top Shelf Series:

Bastards & Whiskey

Villains & Vodka

Scoundrels & Scotch

Devils & Rye

Beasts & Bourbon

Evil Lies Series:

The Truth About Cinder

The Truth About Alice

Delicate Disaster Duet:

Delicate Scars

Delicate Wounds

Dark Fantasy Series:

Snow & the Seven Huntsmen

Red & the Wolves

Queen & the Kingsmen

Kings & Sinners Series:

Maddox

Stryder

Anson

Captive Vow

Bad Bad Girl

Fallen Daughters

Bride to Keep

His Caged Kitty

Bared

Caged

Forbidden

For all of my books, check out my Amazon Page!

http://amzn.to/2CTmeen

Made in the USA
Las Vegas, NV
06 May 2022